BRIE'S SUBMISSION

Whispered Promises

Red Phoenix

Copyright © 2022 Red Phoenix
Print Edition
www.redphoenixauthor.com

Whispered Promises:
Brie's Submission Book 24

Cover by Shanoff Designs
Formatted by BB Books
Phoenix symbol by Nicole Delfs

All rights reserved. Except as permitted under the U.S. Copyright Act of 1976, no part of this publication may be reproduced, distributed, or transmitted in any form or by any means, or stored in a database or retrieval system, without the prior written permission of the author.

Dedication

Forgive me, this is a long one!
(I was feeling all the feels while writing this story and am incredibly thankful)

I dedicate Whispered Promises to my family, my muses, and my friends!

This book has been an incredible journey. I have truly enjoyed it even though I was sweating it there for a bit. You see, my mother almost died while I was writing the book. I cannot express my fear or how hard it was to concentrate on anything. Biggest thanks to MrRed, who was my rock through everything.

Fortunately, my mom is slowly recovering, and I am overcome with relief. I understand that death comes to all of us, but it's still not easy to face losing those you love.

I am incredibly lucky that my husband and my kids fully support my writing. My daughter Jessica came up with the title "Whispered Promises"–which I love–and my son Jon and his partner, Ben (whom I think of as a son) never stopped encouraging me during the writing process. They also came up with all kinds of fun ideas to include my fans while I was neck-deep in writing Whispered Promises.

I always have to give a shout-out to my muses. I still can't believe these incredible people (and they most definitely feel like real people to me) not only share their stories with us, but they also continue to make me laugh, cry, swoon, and gasp every time I write. They are a beautiful part of my life. I am and will always be tremendously honored they chose me!

And a huge thanks to my friends who help make these stories possible. They bless my life in unbelievable ways every day:

Thank you, KH Koehler. I always enjoy your edits and appreciate that your intention is to perfect my words while protecting the story. It is an honor to work with you.

To Pippa Jayne, whom I absolutely adore! Thank you for being the voice for Brie in audio. Your love for the characters shines through in your work. How lucky am I that you have also become a dear friend throughout the years (8 so far - can you believe it?).

Brenda, Becki, Marilyn, and Kennia, I can't tell you how much I appreciate your dedication to the story. You are not only my betas, but my cherished friends. I am so very grateful for you.

Anthony, your support changed the course of my career and allowed me to continue writing the stories I love. Your knowledge, patience, and kindness have made such a huge difference in my life. Thank you for giving me the power to do what I love for many years to come.

Paul, you have worked with me from almost the very beginning. I remember I cried tears of joy after you took over formatting my books. You have had my back for years–through all the many versions of Brie.

Kyle, you not only bless my life with your friendship but also make getting my book out in time possible. In honor of your humor, I have included one of your jokes.

Julia, you were there at the very beginning when I became Red Phoenix. You read my first short stories, starting with "Loving Amy" and "Keeper of the Wolves". You will never know how much your support meant to me then. Your love of life and our friendship is something I am profoundly grateful for!

To all of my fans, I love sharing my muses with you. You literally changed my life by loving my books. I am humbled by every beloved gift you make, every time you reach out to me, and how much you make me smile and laugh every week in my group @FriendsofRedPhoenix.

Your excitement spurs me on, my friends. I am eternally grateful that you are in my life!

Much love,

~Red

SIGN UP FOR MY NEWSLETTER HERE FOR THE LATEST RED PHOENIX UPDATES

FOLLOW ME ON INSTAGRAM

INSTAGRAM.COM/REDPHOENIXAUTHOR

SALES, GIVEAWAYS, NEW RELEASES, PREORDER LINKS, AND MORE!

SIGN UP HERE

REDPHOENIXAUTHOR.COM/NEWSLETTER-SIGNUP

CONTENTS

No Escape

"Hello, Brianna Bennet…"

Brie's blood ran cold when she heard Greg Holloway's voice.

He held her tightly with one hand pressed hard against her mouth. "You are mine now."

Brie struggled against him in a desperate attempt to escape.

He only laughed with amusement. "You can struggle all you want, but there is nothing you can do to change what is about to happen." The tone of his voice became even more ominous. "First, I must teach you your place, and then I will *educate* you."

An imposing man covered in prison tattoos scowled at her as he approached. He yanked Brie's purse from her arm, breaking the strap. Pulling her phone out, he threw it to the floor of the darkened theater before slamming the heel of his boot onto it and shattering the screen.

No one can find me…she thought.

The blood in Brie's ears began to pound as genuine terror took over.

The lights of the theatre suddenly cut through the darkness, disorienting her for a moment. To her dismay, two more towering men walked into the theatre, their eyes locked on her as if she were prey.

Holloway pressed himself against her. "Yes…" he crooned in her ear. "You should be frightened, Miss Bennett. I plan to sit and watch you pay for every indignity I have had to endure because of you."

Greg shouted his next order. "Start the film from the beginning."

The projector started up again.

With sickening glee, Holloway whispered, "These men will not stop until the last credit rolls across the screen. I want you to remember every second of your punishment whenever you watch your 'precious' documentary."

Brie trembled. She understood that Holloway not only wanted to torture her, but also make her associate her beloved film with the perversity about to take place so she could never watch it again.

Goosebumps covered her skin as the three muscular men looked her up and down. Brie could feel the violence of their thoughts when she looked into their eyes. It caused her body to instantly jump into flight mode.

Brie bit down hard on Holloway's fleshy palm and silently rejoiced when he released her. The theatre filled with his high-pitched screams.

Taking advantage of her freedom, Brie ran down between two rows of chairs, heading to the opposite aisle that led to an outdoor exit.

"Don't let her get away!" Holloway shrieked.

Brie's instincts kicked into overdrive as she raced for the door and freedom. Clasping the metal bar, Brie pushed down on it and heard the satisfying click just before the door opened. But, just as the warm light of the sun flooded the theatre, Brie felt her feet leave the ground as she was yanked back inside.

Screaming for help at the top of her lungs, Brie flew through the air like a rag doll, landing hard on the floor with a jolting thud. It knocked the wind out of her, and she lay there momentarily stunned.

Brie felt a massive hand close around her throat as the man with the tattoos dug his fingers into her skin. Lifting her off her feet by her neck, he slammed her against the wall. Brie flailed in desperation, unable to breathe, as Holloway slowly strolled up to her.

Brie noticed blood dripping from his hand, staining the sky-blue carpet. He shook his head slowly as he approached. "You are going to pay *dearly* for that."

Brie suddenly began to see pinpoints of light as her body reacted to the lack of oxygen. Just as she was about to pass out, the man released his hold around her throat and slammed his hand against her chest to keep her upright against the wall.

Holloway waited until she'd caught her breath before slapping her hard on the cheek with his bloody hand. The power of his blow caused her head to snap back, banging her opposite cheek into the wall.

Silencing her moan of pain, Brie turned her head and

glared at him defiantly.

"I like that you still have fight left, Miss Bennett." Holloway smiled, nodding to the front of the stage. "I've reserved a front-row seat for the show."

His grin sickened her.

"You may be insolent now but I promise you will be quite complacent after we are done here."

The man with the tattoos started dragging Brie toward the large screen. Even though she hit him with her fists repeatedly, she was powerless to stop him. Once he lugged her to the front, he forced her to the floor and pressed his foot against her head, crushing her cheek against the floor with the treads of his boot.

Brie was terrified but stilled the whimpers that threatened to escape, not wanting to give Holloway the satisfaction. She watched in disgust as he settled down in a chair just a few feet away from her and said with a glint in his eye, "You won't be the same after they've finished with you, Miss Bennett. I've instructed them not to hold back."

The other two men surrounded her, grunting in anticipation as they ripped off their shirts and glowered at her.

Brie closed her eyes tightly and silently cried out for Sir.

Although she wanted to be brave, tears rolled down her cheeks despite her best efforts to hold them back. The moment Holloway saw them, he chortled in delight. "I can't wait for the sweet sound of your cries for mercy, Miss Bennett. But there will be no mercy for you…"

"I'll keep her still," the man holding her down with

his boot told the others.

To Brie, he commanded, "Open your eyes."

When she refused, he ground his boot against her cheek. The excruciating pain made it feel like her cheekbone was about to give under the weight.

She opened her eyes to find him staring down at her. His dark eyes drilled into her when he stated, "I'll make sure you can't move. Then, after the others are finished, I'll introduce you to my own style of 'play'."

When she felt someone tugging on her clothes, she started screaming, "No!" at the top of her lungs. But her desperate cries were only met with their low laughter.

She realized there would be no escape from this…

Brie held on to her love for Thane and her two babies, trying to block everything else out while her clothes were methodically ripped from her body. It took a moment for her brain to register the far-off sound.

She opened her eyes to see that all three men were frozen in fear.

Holding her breath, Brie felt a flood of relief when she recognized the shrill sound of sirens in the distance.

"Are they coming for us?" one of the men asked Holloway, sounding agitated.

Holloway shook his head and scoffed. "They're headed in the other direction, you idiot."

The man covered in tattoos growled. "No, they're not. The sirens are coming closer."

All three men looked at each other.

"I'm not going back to jail, fucker!" the other man barked at Holloway.

Keeping his boot firmly on her cheek, the man holding Brie down growled fiercely, "You promised no one would know we were here."

"Nobody does!" Holloway insisted.

Pointing in the direction of the sirens, he snarled, "It doesn't sound like it to me. I'm out!"

Lifting his boot from Brie's face, he headed to the exit with the other two following behind him.

"You can't leave!" Holloway shouted. "This bitch needs to be punished!"

The tatted man turned back and growled, "Then do it yourself, you fat fuck."

Brie took advantage of their exchange and scooted as far away from Holloway as she could. Not caring that she was completely naked, Brie stood up and sprinted toward the exit door.

Holloway called out to her in a voice as cold as ice, "If you go out that door, I will kill Mary."

Brie stopped in her tracks, knowing with certainty that he would.

With her heart breaking, she turned away from her freedom to face him. "Don't you dare hurt her."

The kid in the ticket booth burst into the theatre, his voice cracking when he screamed at Holloway, "The cops are heading this way! Follow me, I know a way out."

Holloway grabbed Brie's arm and followed the boy. He led them to the front of the stage and opened a hidden panel. "This tunnel goes underneath the theatre. If you take the first turn to the left, it will lead you straight to the Spielberg Theatre. They won't be looking for you there."

"Grab her clothes!" Holloway ordered.

The boy rushed over to pick up the scattered clothing and then raced back, tossing them into the tunnel. "You gotta go!"

In a calm voice, Holloway instructed him, "Escape out the back and drive home. If the cops question you, tell them the theatre was closed for maintenance. The owner will back up your story."

Holloway pushed Brie toward the tunnel as he continued, "Lock the front door, grab the bitch's phone and purse, and turn everything off before you head out the back exit."

Turning to Brie, Holloway spoke over the sirens that were now wailing loudly. "I planned for every situation. Understand that if anything happens to me, Mary's life is forfeit and she won't die quickly."

Letting Brie go, Holloway grabbed her clothes scattered in the tunnel and shouted at her, "Go now!"

Brie's heart was beating out of her chest as she started down the darkened tunnel. Her fear of dark, confined spaces was intensified by the surreal aspect of what was happening. Here she was, willingly remaining Holloway's captive, even though rescue was just moments away.

But she would never forgive herself if Mary died…

"To the left! To the left!" Holloway growled, panting heavily behind her.

As Brie made her way down the tunnel, cobwebs clung to her naked body making her skin crawl. She tried desperately not to think about the spiders that had created them.

The sound of the sirens blared behind her filling Brie

with hope. But it was tempered by knowing that if they *were* found, Mary would end up paying the price. Either way, Holloway would win.

It filled her with rage.

Brie heard the muffled sounds of people shouting behind them. She imagined the police bursting into the theatre but finding nothing. She could only hope they would find the drops of blood on the carpet and know that Holloway had been there.

She couldn't fathom how Sir had been able to locate them after Holloway had broken her phone. It seemed impossible, but she felt certain he was the one who had tracked them down.

Brie imagined Sir searching every inch of the theatre hoping to find her. Tears pricked her eyes realizing how devastated he would be when his search came up empty.

Don't give up! she silently cried out. *Mary and I need you.*

When Brie finally made it to the other theatre, Holloway threw her clothes at her. "Get dressed. I can't have you drawing any attention."

With shaking hands, Brie only slipped her dress over her head after she found her bra and panties were ripped and unusable. She shuddered, knowing that would have been the state of her body if it hadn't been for the sound of the sirens.

Before leaving the tunnel, Holloway pulled out a cheap looking cell phone and called someone, "Meet me at the corner of Selma and McCadden in ten minutes, and don't go anywhere near the Egyptian entrance."

Once outside, Holloway slammed the phone to the ground and crushed it with his heel. He nonchalantly tossed it in a nearby dumpster before grabbing Brie's arm. "Although I did not get the entertainment of seeing you punished, I do get perverse satisfaction in knowing that you are *choosing* to stay with me. I'm certain in the days ahead that decision will eat you alive." He nodded with a self-satisfied grin on his face. "Yes, it is fitting that you will come to blame yourself for what is about to happen."

"What are you talking about?" she asked, now terrified.

"Your training is about to begin, Miss Bennett. By the time I'm done, you will willingly offer yourself to the likes of those three men and take pleasure in their violation because it pleases me."

Brie hissed. "Never!"

His smile broadened. "You say that now, songbird. However, you will soon be singing a much different tune."

Brie stared at him in disbelief. "You're delusional!"

His eyes darkened and he raised his hand to strike her. But, after studying Brie for a moment, he seemed to have second thoughts and lowered it.

Cocking his head to one side, Holloway smiled coldly. "I will take extreme pleasure in teaching you to respect me, Miss Bennett."

"I will *never* respect you."

He chuckled coldly. "You will come to eat those words."

When Brie met his hostile gaze, fear began to worm its way back into her heart. Mary's warning suddenly rang in her head. *"You have no idea what you have unleashed, and I have no way to stop him now."*

Swallowing hard, Brie recalled the numerous times Mary had warned her that Holloway was exceedingly cunning and cruel. She had never taken it seriously—until she looked into his eyes just now.

Brie was hit with the cold realization…

On the night of her triumph in Hollywood, she'd mistakenly believed she'd won by taking Holloway down in front of his peers.

The truth was she had only awakened the beast, and now she and Mary were about to suffer for it in unimaginable ways.

Captive

Holloway kept a tight arm around Brie until they were safely in the vehicle and miles away from the theatre.

When the driver handed back a new phone, Holloway finally let go of Brie and sat back in his seat. With a sickening smirk, he began texting furiously.

Once again, Brie was struck by the surreal nature of her capture. When his driver pulled onto the avenue and they were stopped by traffic, she looked out the window at a family in the car beside her. She saw a little girl with blonde hair in the back seat staring at her intently. The girl reminded her of Mary.

Brie was desperate to cry out for help when the father turned to look in her direction, but she kept silent when she glanced back at the little girl—she couldn't risk Mary's life.

Holloway ordered his man to pull into an alley and informed him, "We're transferring vehicles."

"Venom will help you out," Holloway barked to Brie

without looking back as he exited the vehicle and slammed the door behind him. The car rocked from the force.

Brie froze when a skinny man climbed out of the dark van in front of her and started walking toward the vehicle. He had a dark countenance that terrified her.

The man had a strange tattoo peeking out of the collar of his shirt. As he approached, she realized it was the head of a large cobra looking like it was ready to strike.

Brie could not explain it, but this man terrified her on an instinctual level she'd never experienced before.

When he opened the car door and nodded toward the van, Brie hesitated—petrified to leave the safety of the vehicle.

The look he gave her chilled her to the bone. The moment she got out of the vehicle, he threw a black hood over her head and tightened the drawstring around her neck, stating, "You are *his* property now."

The weight behind those words paralyzed her. Still, she cried out, "Never!"

He leaned closer, warning in a deadly tone, "Every time you speak, Mary Wilson will be punished."

Brie gasped, offering no further resistance when he grabbed her wrists and cuffed them behind her back. As soon as the man pushed her into the van and slid the door shut behind him, it lurched forward.

She could hear Holloway cussing up a storm in the front seat. It was obvious he was still rattled by the unexpected interruption at the Egyptian Theatre. He hadn't anticipated it, which proved he wasn't as clever as he thought.

Brie knew Sir would find her again, and she held on desperately to that hope in the hours that followed as they drove farther and farther away from LA…

The van didn't stop until late that night. The instant the driver threw the vehicle into park, Brie heard Holloway mutter, "You know what to do, Venom."

When the van door slid open, Brie was confronted by the heavy humidity in the air. It clung to her skin as it invaded her lungs, making it hard to breathe under the hood.

Strong hands grabbed Brie's ankles and yanked her out of the van. She fell to the wet ground, grunting in pain. The earthy scent of a forest filled her nostrils as the terrifying man named Venom pulled her back to her feet and uncuffed her.

"Strip," he growled.

"No."

Her defiance was met with a hard backhand to her face, making Brie gasp in pain.

He replied darkly, "How much do you want her to suffer?"

She realized he was talking about Mary, and instantly regretted her decision. With trembling hands, she slipped out of her dress, resigning herself to her current fate.

To protect Mary, Brie knew she had to play out this repulsive role Holloway had set for her. But Greg Holloway had always failed to appreciate how strong she was. Whatever he had planned, she would not only survive it but would escape from his clutches, taking Mary with her.

Until then, Brie's sole focus was to continue playing along to protect Mary and give Sir the time he needed to locate them.

Venom grasped her arm tightly as he marched her down a muddy path. The cold mud was so slippery that her bare feet could find no traction and she fell several times. Each time she slipped, Venom jerked her back to her feet and berated her.

Brie stiffened when she heard Holloway's low chuckle behind her. It seared her soul to know he enjoyed watching her struggle.

Although the hood still covered her head, Brie held her chin high in defiance of the man. It was foolish of Holloway to think he could ever break her!

Brie cried out when she unexpectedly stubbed her toe on the first step of a flight of stairs. She ignored the pain as Venom forced her up the remaining steps and she heard the creak of a door as it opened.

The instant she walked inside, Brie was enveloped by warmth as the sound of burning logs crackled nearby her.

She was shocked to hear people casually talking to each other in what seemed a party setting. They took no notice of her and their conversations continued uninterrupted while she was led past them.

It was as if seeing a naked girl with a hood over her head was a common occurrence for these people.

Her heart skipped a beat when she was suddenly reminded of the night in Russia when a slaver had brought Stephanie to the sadists' dungeon. He'd offered to sell her to anyone interested in buying the girl. The man had treated Stephanie as if she were simply property, abusing her in front of everyone to show how obedient she was.

But that night, the slaver paid the ultimate price for his mistake when Rytsar exacted his justice and rescued Stephanie from the man.

By the sound of the party atmosphere going on around Brie, she got the distinct impression that no one here was concerned about her or her fate—it was horrifying to feel invisible when she was desperate for help.

After being led down a flight of stairs and dragged down a long hallway, Brie could no longer hear the people above her. The air was much colder in the basement, causing goosebumps to rise on her naked skin.

Venom stopped to open a door and ordered her inside. When she didn't immediately comply, he pushed her inside and ripped the hood off her head.

She had expected to see a dungeon cell, and it certainly had that feeling when she saw the chains with metal cuffs on the far wall and the large cage in the corner. However, the room also had a luxurious king-sized bed, along with a roaring fire.

As inviting as the fire was, Brie felt a cold chill run down her spine. She was certain terrible things had taken place in the room, and every cell in her body was telling her to run.

Glancing at the open door behind her, she was severely tempted to bolt.

Venom made no move to stop her. Instead, he asked one simple question, "How much do you want Mary Wilson to suffer?"

Brie shuddered, closing her eyes as she let out a defeated sigh. If she wanted Mary to survive, she must wait to be rescued.

Slowly turning to Venom, she answered, "I do not want Mary to suffer."

Brie shivered in fear when he said with a cruel glint in his eye, "Let the breaking begin, then."

Venom pointed to the large cage. Brie's gaze darted to the strange metal structure styled like a birdcage.

He walked to it and opened the door.

Dread filled her heart. The idea of willingly giving up her freedom to Holloway went against everything she believed in. But, she understood the role she must play and stepped inside.

Venom slammed the door shut and pulled out a key, locking her inside the cage. He scowled at her through the bars, stating in contempt, "You are less than nothing."

Dousing the fire, he turned off the light in the room before walking out. The moment the door shut, Brie was enshrouded in inky darkness.

Without the fire, the room quickly became cold.

Ever since she was a child, Brie had been afraid of dark, confined places and she was unable to stop the suffocating fear that gripped her heart now. Out of desperation, she grabbed the bars and started shaking the door of the cage, needing to get out.

Brie suddenly stopped herself, realizing that Holloway had probably installed cameras in the room to document her every move. She was certain he was taking great pleasure in seeing how terrified she was right now.

Taking several deep breaths, Brie let go of the bars and slid down onto the cold floor. She closed her eyes and concentrated on her breathing. It took a long time, but she eventually felt the warmth of Tono's calming spirit as it began to flood her soul.

Alone in the dark, Brie had no sense of time. Being constantly cold did not allow her the escape of falling asleep. Instead, she wrapped her arms around herself and forced herself to think about Hope and Antony. She missed them so deeply that it was difficult for her to hold back the tears.

But Brie held onto the knowledge that Sir was doing everything possible to find her, and she was certain that Rytsar had already mobilized his men in the US to aid Sir in those efforts.

Try as she might, however, the utter silence in the pitch-black room began to mess with her head. It sickened her to think of the foul things that must have taken place in this room.

It felt as if the evil of this place was swirling around her, waiting to consume her.

Brie wondered if Mary was close by, sitting alone in the dark, thinking she had been abandoned by the world.

She cried out loud, "Hold on, Mary! Help is coming. Don't give in to the darkness."

Brie had no concept of how much time had passed, but it was long enough that her unbearable hunger was slowly being driven out by her intense thirst.

She licked her dry lips and shivered in the darkness, wondering when rescue would come. She'd begun daydreaming about water. But her thirst, combined with the cold, kept demanding her attention and left her no escape from the torment.

When she finally heard footsteps approach the door, Brie felt both relief and dread.

She tensed in fear when the door opened, and then cringed when bright white light filled the room. It physically hurt, like looking into the sun, and she whimpered as she buried her head in her arms.

The footsteps continued until the man stopped in front of the cage.

Holding her breath, Brie wondered if Venom had come to torment her further. Instead, she heard Holloway ask, "Are you thirsty?"

Even though she thoroughly hated the man, Brie nodded without lifting her head.

Her heart skipped a beat when she heard him unlock the cage. She lifted her head and squinted in the bright light while the door slowly swung open.

Brie was surprised to see Holloway holding out a glass of water to her.

When she reached out to take it, he chuckled and took several steps back. "No, you do not get the honor of drinking from the glass."

She frowned in confusion.

"First, you will bow at my feet. Then, you must beg for it."

Brie's eyes narrowed. "I will not beg to the likes of you."

Holloway sneered. "You've always failed to give me the respect I deserved, but I will teach you to grovel like a good slave."

Brie rolled her eyes. "That will *never* happen."

He raised an eyebrow, saying with confidence, "You will be surprised at the things I can make you do."

Raising her chin higher, she told him, "It won't be long until my husband comes—just like he did at the theatre. Thane will stop at nothing to find me, and with Rytsar Durov by his side, I can guarantee your life will be forfeit."

"You are a fool, but you always have been," Holloway said condescendingly. "There is a whole underworld you know nothing about. This compound is off the grid. Only a select few know it even exists, and every person here would die to protect me. But, you? You have no worth here. You are but chattel to them. I could snap your neck right now simply for the fun of it and no one would care."

Brie was frightened, certain he was telling her the truth, but she continued to stare at him defiantly.

Holloway chuckled. "Ah, I see you still believe you have value. Rest assured, I will strip that from you layer by layer." His eyes grew dark when he added, "And I will enjoy every moment of your awakening."

Songbird

Before leaving her, Holloway tipped back the glass of water and drank every drop while she watched. Afterward, he swept his hand over his mouth and winked at her.

The entire cage rattled when he shut the door and slid the key in to lock it. He smiled as he looked at the metal bars. "Do you know why I chose a birdcage for you?"

Brie stared at him but said nothing.

"You are my songbird." He glanced at the bed, his laughter low and cruel. "I can't wait to hear your guttural songs of passion when I claim you."

Bile rose in her throat.

Holloway quickly turned and shut off the light before closing the door behind him. She was grateful to hear his footsteps echo down the hallway as he walked away. But soon, all she heard was silence. Once again, she was alone in the smothering darkness.

She couldn't stop replaying the image of Holloway

drinking the water in front of her, and it left her even thirstier than before.

Brie struggled to hold back her tears, unsure how she would survive another day.

"Don't give up," she called to Mary as she laid her head against the bars of the cage and closed her eyes.

Brie screamed out loud when music suddenly filled the room. A low, seductive male voice began singing, "Hey, little songbird…"

The dark undertones of the lyrics seemed to match the man's dangerous voice, causing goosebumps to rise on Brie's skin. It was like listening to a predator singing to its next meal.

When Brie heard the beautiful voice of a woman taking over, she thought it would provide much-needed relief, but the girl sang about wanting to feed out of the man's hand.

Brie covered her ears, frightened by the meaning behind the lyrics, but the music was so loud that she could still hear every word. The song reverberated around her like a physical force, making Brie its unwilling captive.

When Holloway finally returned, Brie was on the verge of a panic attack.

The moment he opened the door, the music stopped. He turned on the light and walked over to the cage, chuckling lightly. "I see the music has had an effect on you."

Brie was grateful for the unexpected silence and took several deep breaths, trying to calm herself. Once her eyes adjusted to the bright light, she noticed the glass of water Holloway held in his hand as he walked to the large bed. He placed the glass on a nightstand.

Brie couldn't stop staring at it, captivated by the idea of the cold water traveling down her parched throat. When Holloway caught her eying the glass, he asked with an almost playful grin, "Would you like a drink?"

She assumed he was teasing her but nodded anyway.

Holloway walked over to unlocked the cage, opening the door wide before returning to sit on the bed.

"You know what you must do."

Brie swallowed hard. The only way she could survive was to submit to his games. Slowly pushing herself up off the floor, she stood on unsteady legs and walked out of the cage.

Holloway watched her with interest but made no move to help her when she stumbled only a few feet away from him. The entire time, Brie kept her eyes riveted on the glass of water.

When she reached out a shaking hand to take it, he shook his head.

Sighing in resignation, she lowered herself to the floor and bowed before him.

"Forehead on the concrete," he ordered.

Even though it killed her inside, Brie reminded herself that she was not submitting to him but to her need for water. This was simply a role she was being forced to play.

Placing her palms on the floor in front of her in supplication, Brie pressed her forehead against the cold floor.

"And, now…?" he stated.

Brie sighed inwardly, hating that he was making her

beg, but she forced the words out of her parched throat, "Please, may I have a drink of water?"

He scoffed. "Look at me."

The last thing she wanted to do was to look at that hated man's face, but she lifted her head and gazed into his eyes, repeating, "Please, may I have a drink of water?"

He cupped his hand and poured some of the water from the glass into his palm, then held it out to her. "Drink."

Brie watched in desperation as the water seeped through his fingers and fell onto the floor.

"You must earn the honor of drinking from the glass," he stated, pouring more water into his palm.

Her instinctual need suddenly took over and she grasped his hand, sucking up the water from his palm before it was all lost.

Holloway poured more water and watched in satisfaction as Brie drank from his hand again. "Little songbird."

She bristled at the name and pulled away from him. But the moment Holloway filled his palm again, she returned to it. Her need for water overrode everything else. When the glass was empty, Brie sat back on her heels, shivering and still thirsty.

He looked pleased and announced to her, "Tomorrow, I will take you to see Mary."

She glanced up at him. "Is she okay?"

Holloway ignored the question and commanded, "Get back in the cage."

Brie reluctantly stood up and returned to the metal

cage. She felt disheartened when she heard the clank of the metal as he shut the cage door and locked it.

Holloway walked out without saying another word. He turned off the lights and shut the door without glancing back at her.

Brie was eternally grateful that the music did not start up again. But, to her horror, the song continued to play in her head while the silence settled around her.

As the lyrics continued and the girl began to sing, goosebumps rose on Brie's skin. In her head, she heard: "Strange is the call of this strange man. I want to fly down and feed at his hand…"

It felt eerily similar to what had just happened with the water. Brie began rocking herself, remembering what Holloway had said.

You will be surprised at the things I can make you do…

The Party

Having no concept of time, it felt like an eternity before Brie heard the footsteps return. But, instead of Holloway, Venom entered the room.

After turning on the light, he strode up to the cage. Brie felt a sense of dread and backed away from the door when he unlocked it.

"Out!" he commanded.

She hesitated and immediately paid the consequence. Reaching into the cage, he grabbed her arm, his fingers digging painfully into her skin as he dragged her out. "Disobedience has its price."

Brie flinched, expecting he would hit her, but he pushed her out of the room instead. She had to struggle to keep up with him as Venom walked briskly down the hallway.

He didn't stop until they came to a gray door. "Go in."

Brie had no idea what was on the other side of the door but she opened it, hoping to see Mary.

Instead, she saw two girls waiting for her. Neither spoke to Brie, but they directed her to follow them as they led her to a large shower stall. Brie looked down at her skin, still covered in the dried mud that clung to her from that first night.

How many days had it been since then?

Brie didn't have time to think as the two girls made quick work of her, scrubbing the mud from her body before thoroughly washing her skin and hair.

While they were toweling her off, Brie whispered, "My name is Brianna Davis. What are your names?"

Neither girl responded. When she tried again, they shook their heads, looking at her fearfully.

Brie felt chills when she realized they must be captives like her.

One of the girls brought her a white garment. Brie thanked her as she slipped it over her head. The material was so thin, however, that it was almost see-through and provided no warmth. She recognized the clothing was not for her benefit but Holloway's.

After drying and brushing out her hair, the two women escorted her to the door. Before she left, Brie said under her breath, "Rescue is coming."

Venom stood just outside the door. Brie noticed one of the girls holding up four fingers to him.

He grunted, then glared at Brie.

Brie's heart began to race, wondering what it meant.

Without saying a word, Venom led her up the long flight of stairs. Brie could hear people casually chatting above. From out of nowhere, she was hit by a terrible feeling and immediately stopped in her tracks.

A cruel smile played on his lips as Venom gripped her arm and forced her up the rest of the stairs.

When they reached the top, Brie was assaulted by the delicious smell of rich foods. Her stomach grumbled loudly in protest. She glanced around the room and saw waiters offering fancy hors d'oeuvres and various wines to guests.

It was surreal…

"Ah, the entertainment has arrived!" Holloway stated excitedly as he walked up to Brie.

All eyes suddenly turned in her direction and Brie could feel a sense of anticipation rising in the room. The thin material of her clothing made Brie feel exposed, which she knew was exactly what Holloway wanted.

When he put his arm around Brie, her skin crawled.

That feeling of danger she'd experienced before only increased as she listened to him address the crowd. "This is a rare treat for me, and I am gratified to all of you for coming tonight to enjoy this moment with me."

Brie nervously scanned the room hoping to see Mary. What she saw made the blood drain from her face. Darius was standing with a group of men, laughing loudly as he grabbed a canapé from a waiter passing by.

Darius must have felt the intensity of her stare because he suddenly looked up and met her gaze. Without missing a beat, he took another morsel from the tray and smiled at her as he popped it in his mouth and chewed it slowly.

Brie's stomach twisted in knots. She'd never experienced such a deep level of betrayal.

Seeing him triggered memories of his abuse when

she was younger, and she suddenly found herself struggling to breathe.

"Ah, yes," Holloway said, obviously pleased by her reaction. "Darius wouldn't be where he is today if it weren't for me."

"Friends!" Holloway shouted gleefully beside her, "The time has come."

Holloway led Brie down the hall to a large room lined with chairs. She bit her lip to hold back her scream when she saw Mary, dressed in the same garment, bound face-first to a St Andrew's cross in the center of the room.

People flooded in, chatting excitedly as they took their seats.

Holloway leaned over to Brie and whispered, "The time has come for your education, songbird."

Dread washed over Brie as she watched Venom stand beside the cross and take off his shirt. She stared at the large tattoo of the cobra that coiled around his body. It looked to Brie as if the cobra was about to strike her dead.

It was grotesquely fascinating because it was a perfect match to the menacing aura he gave off.

Brie whimpered when Venom picked up a studded whip and approached Mary. He ripped at the thin material of Mary's garment to expose her back.

Venom then lightly grazed his hand over her pristine skin and turned to Brie, stating in an authoritative tone, "Every action has an equal and opposite reaction."

She watched in horror as he took his stance behind Mary and raised the evil-looking whip.

"Stop!" Brie cried when he raised the whip to strike. "I'm the one who should be punished."

Mary jerked in her chains when she heard Brie's voice.

Venom turned his head, saying with a cruel smile. "So, you want to add one more?"

Brie covered her mouth with both her hands, realizing her outburst had just cost Mary another lash.

Holloway left Brie's side and slowly walked around the cross as he told her, "I know how you tick, songbird. You've spent your whole life making connections with people, attempting to build a 'family' of sorts." He reached out and stroked Mary's blonde hair. "You even managed to win over my most prized possession."

He looked back at Brie. "Of course, I could have Venom punish you for everything you've done, but…" Holloway's gaze bore into her when he added, "I know you."

Glancing at Mary again, he smiled. "You will feel every lash she takes as if it were cutting your own skin. But it will hurt even more because she will be taking the punishment meant for you."

Tears ran down Brie's face, helpless to stop what was about to happen.

Venom resumed his position behind Mary and pulled back his arm. "The first one is for speaking without permission." Brie watched in horror as the tails whipped through the air. The sickening sound of the metal studs making contact with Mary's skin filled the air. Somehow, Mary held back her screams and didn't make a sound.

"The second is refusing a command."

She silently cried out as Mary took another powerful lash that made the chains rattle. Sinking to the floor, Brie sobbed as she watched the welts swell on Mary's back as blood slowly trickled down.

Holloway held up his hand to stop Venom, and asked Brie, "What would you do to spare her?"

She immediately rushed to Holloway and bowed low at his feet, crushing her forehead against the floor. "Let me take my punishment. I beg you to spare Mary."

He chuckled angrily. "I thought you said you would never beg to 'the likes of me'."

Brie choked back her tears. "I was wrong."

"You were wrong about so many things, songbird." Holloway waved his hand in the air dismissively and said to Venom, "Continue."

A few seconds later, Brie heard Venom call out, "This is for not obeying fast enough to a command."

Holloway pulled Brie to her feet and forced her to watch as Mary received the next lash. She knew that particular lash was for her hesitation when Venom had ordered her out of the cage.

I'm so sorry, Mary…

"The next four are for speaking to others."

When Brie saw Mary tense, her heart broke.

This was all her fault. She had tried twice to get the girls' names while they were bathing her, and just before she left them, she told them rescue was coming. But she hadn't spoken four times. Had the girls added an extra one just to be cruel?

Then she remembered thanking one of the girls when she handed Brie the cover she was now wearing.

It gutted her to know Mary was paying dearly for that simple mistake. She held her breath as Mary took the four lashes in rapid succession. Unable to hold back any longer, Mary cried out in unbearable pain and then slumped against her bindings.

"Stand," Venom barked.

When Mary didn't respond, he walked up to her and slapped her face several times. "There's no escaping your fate tonight."

Holloway grinned as he watched Mary struggle to stand up. He turned to Brie, his smile growing wider. "This is all on you, songbird."

Brie regretted begging Venom to stop as she watched him return to his stance.

"Make it extra hard," Holloway instructed. "We don't want this lesson to be forgotten."

Brie's lip trembled as Venom pulled back his arm to deliver the final lash. She glanced at the crowd who were eagerly watching Mary's punishment. Some of the men were even stroking themselves in excitement.

It made Brie physically ill.

She lowered her eyes, but Holloway immediately reprimanded her. "Focus on your punishment, songbird."

Brie reluctantly looked up, not wanting to cause Mary any more pain than she already had. She held her breath as Venom wound up for the final lash.

The man smiled as he released his wrath on Mary. She let out a scream that filled the room, and Brie's back exploded in agony as if she were taking the lash herself.

Venom stepped away with a satisfied expression on his face while Brie listened to the men around her grunting in release.

Holloway put his hand on Brie's shoulder and turned her to face the people he had invited. "Meet my new slave. As you can see, she was a willful cunt but understands her place now."

As if to prove it, he ordered Brie, "Strip for the fine people."

She could not risk Mary being punished anymore and slid off the garment without hesitation.

"Turn so they can see how perfect your skin is compared to your friend."

The shame Brie experienced was overshadowed by the guilt she felt as she complied with his command.

Holloway leaned toward her and ordered, "Kiss me."

When she heard Mary moan in pain behind her, Brie closed her eyes and pressed her lips against his without question even though her stomach twisted in response to the unholy contact.

Holloway grabbed the back of her head and kissed her harder before letting go. Brie stumbled backward, startled when she heard everyone clapping around her.

"Do you hear that?" Holloway whispered in her ear. "They approve of the change in you, songbird. Maybe we will reward them next time."

Holloway nodded to Venom, who quickly unbound Mary. She fell into her torturer's arms, too weak and in pain to support herself. As they passed by, Brie instinctively reached out to her.

Mary turned her head, hissing at Brie. "Stay the fuck away from me, bitch!"

Holloway teased Mary. "There's no need for jealousy, pet. I'm man enough to satisfy you both."

The room broke out in amused laughter at Mary's expense.

Holloway turned to Brie and added smugly, "If there's one thing I know, it's how to put cunts in their place."

Whispers

Venom returned a short time later. He was leading twelve young women and men with him. They were all dressed in the same see-through covers Brie had been wearing.

Holloway smiled broadly, telling his guests, "As promised, the main course has arrived. Feel free to partake and enjoy. They live to please."

Brie felt sick. Venom grabbed her arm and ordered her to follow. She went without protest, not wanting to give the man any excuse to punish Mary further. On her way out of the large room, she noticed Darius watching her intently.

The weight of his gaze felt like another violation. Instead of cowering under it, she walked past him staring straight ahead and pretended he didn't exist. She would never allow Darius to have another piece of her soul.

Venom didn't speak as he led her back to the basement, but it was obvious by his countenance that he was still riding the high of Mary's brutal punishment. The man wasn't a sadist by any stretch of the imagination. He fed off the pain of others like a leech, offering nothing in return.

As they walked down the hallway, Brie wondered if there were other slaves behind the doors they passed. Until tonight, she'd never imagined there were others locked in this dungeon.

We are here, Sir! She cried out silently, hoping he could sense her. The desperate thought echoed in her head, *There are so many of us depending on you…*

Venom directed Brie into the room and pointed at the cage. As she made her way to it, he glowered at her. "You are less than nothing. You have no voice. If you forget that again, I will personally burn a hole in your tongue to remind you."

Brie shuddered as he shut the cage door and locked it.

After he turned off the light, Venom added, "You exist only to please, in whatever shape or form he decides. Even if it means your death."

Brie whimpered while she listened to his boots echoing down the hallway. She thought back to Mary and her stomach twisted into painful knots. Brie replayed every lash that Mary had suffered, reliving the horrifying sound as the studded tails tore at her back.

How could her friend ever forgive her when every lash was directly linked to something Brie did or failed to do?

She felt overwhelmed by Mary's suffering, but was too dehydrated for a single tear to fall.

Brie could feel her body getting weaker and was unsure how long she could survive like this. Lying on the cement floor, she thought of Rytsar locked in the cell in Siberia. He had survived, despite impossible odds.

I need your strength, Rytsar! she cried silently.

After not sleeping since her arrival, Brie eventually fell into a blessedly deep but troubled sleep.

She laughed with joy, finding herself alone in a vast field of flowers. She soaked in the warmth of the sun under an impossibly blue sky. It was glorious!

Brie had never felt so at peace. Her soul drank up the rays of the sun, as a slight breeze teased her skin. Desperate for more, Brie shimmied out of her sundress and laid it beside her.

Smiling up at the sky, she watched a playful cloud slowly float across the wide expanse of blue. Wanting to feel more of the sun's warmth, Brie undid her bra and slipped off the straps, exposing her breasts to the sunlight.

Greedy for warmth, she eventually pulled off her lace panties and lay back amongst the wildflowers, a smile of contentment on her face. This was pure heaven…

Reacting to the light breeze, her nipples hardened. Looking around to make sure she was alone, Brie reached over to graze her nipple with her fingers. She moaned lightly, delighted by the tiny bolts of electricity that traveled straight to her groin.

It was so pleasurable that she soon began playing with both nipples. She lightly rolled them between her fingers before pulling on them teasingly. She imagined it was Sir's talented touch.

The gentle play made her pussy increasingly wet.

Responding to that need, Brie slipped one hand between her legs.

She leisurely swirled her fingers around her clit, her natural juices making it pleasantly slippery. Brie continued to play with one nipple while she teased her pussy mercilessly.

As if on cue, Sir settled down between her legs to lap up her excitement. "So good…" he murmured just before he began teasing her clit with his tongue.

Brie placed a hand on his head, moaning in delight.

"You like that?" he growled huskily.

"I do, Sir…"

Brie glanced up at the sky and smiled at the wispy cloud. It was the only witness to this glorious moment. When Sir placed his hand just below her stomach and pressed down, it added a higher level of sensual excitement.

"Lie still, babygirl."

Brie joyfully obeyed, closing her eyes as she savored the skill of his tongue. Sir knew how to bring her to the edge, then pull back enough to bring her down before teasing her clit again. He understood that building up to her climax made the eventual release even more intense and pleasurable.

Brie tugged on her nipple a little harder, eliciting delightful sparks of electricity that made her even wetter.

"You taste good, babygirl."

She moaned in pleasure, soaking in his intense love for her as he made sweet love to her pussy with his mouth.

"I thirst for you," she cried out softly.

He lifted his head and smiled hungrily as he stared at her from between her legs. Sitting up, Sir took her in his arms, crushing her against his masculine body as he claimed her lips.

Brie purred when he explored her mouth with his tongue. She could taste her wetness on his lips, and it turned her on even more.

"I love you, babygirl," he murmured huskily.

Brie felt him press his rigid cock against her. Longing to feel him inside her, she begged, "Take me."

"Do you promise not to come?"

She bit her bottom lip, knowing it would be exceedingly difficult. Even so, she vowed, "Yes…"

He reached down to position his cock against her opening but didn't make a move as he looked into her eyes. "How much do you trust me?"

She looked up at him and answered with a full heart, "Completely, Sir."

Sir let out a low, rumbling grunt as he thrust his cock into her. Brie cried out in ecstasy as he filled her with his shaft. She needed that connection with him so desperately that tears sprang to her eyes.

"Don't cry, babygirl." His lips descended on hers, ravaging her mouth while he claimed her body.

Brie wrapped her legs around him, taking him even deep. She let out a cry of satisfaction when he ramped up his strokes, making everything else fade away as she gave in to the challenge of his hard thrusts.

The deep love she felt for Sir was as powerful as his thrusts, keeping her focused solely on him. The intense connection was exactly what she needed, and she moaned in pleasure, teetering on the edge.

"You must wait…" he reminded her.

To help her keep that promise, Sir pulled out and changed position, rubbing his cock against her clit to tease her.

"Close your eyes."

Brie obeyed, a sensual smile on her lips. She savored his touch as he grazed his fingers lightly over her skin. But, she gasped in surprise when she felt another man's lips encasing her nipple as he began to suck.

Turned on by the unexpected stimulation, her pussy began to pulse in response. She was dangerously close to climaxing.

"Help…" she whimpered, knowing she was about to disobey Sir's direct command.

Instead of helping, Sir ramped up the challenge by thrusting his cock back into her. Brie let out a passionate scream, her consciousness on the precipice of sexual nirvana—ready to make the leap and climax without his permission.

She felt the pressure of Rytsar's teeth pressing against her throat while Sir's thrusts became deeper as he gave the guttural command, "You…must…wait."

Brie opened her eyes and looked up at the blue sky while the two men made passionate love to her body amid the field of wildflowers. She was momentarily distracted by a small bird singing its beautiful song as it flitted by her.

A dark shadow suddenly appeared from above.

Before Brie could cry out in warning, a raptor swooped down with its sharp talons and carried the small bird away.

Promise

Brie cried out and woke with a start.

The dream had been so real she could still feel Sir's presence and the pressure of Rytsar's teeth on her neck. She whimpered in the dark, the loss of connection eating at her.

"Pleasant dream?"

Chills coursed through Brie's body at the hated sound of Holloway's voice. She stared into the pitch-black but could see nothing.

Sitting up, Brie scooted to the far side of the cage.

"I have something for you."

Holloway turned on the lamp on the nightstand, forcing Brie to shield her eyes from the sudden light.

"The cage is unlocked. You must bow at my feet to receive it."

She squinted, still adjusting to the light, and saw that Holloway had not only brought a glass of water but a small tray of fruit.

Tears pricked her eyes. The need for sustenance felt

like a physical pain clawing at her insides.

When she failed to move, he barked, "Come now or suffer the consequence."

Sir's words from the dream played in her head. "*You must wait.*"

Brie looked longingly at the water and food. She knew she must survive long enough for Sir to rescue her—whatever the cost.

Feeling light-headed, Brie crawled on all fours to Holloway and pressed her forehead to the floor. This was not an act of surrender but survival.

"Excellent, songbird."

Brie shuddered, remembering what happened to the songbird in her dream. She had no illusions about who Holloway was.

"Turn and kneel, facing away from me."

Her heart racing, Brie followed his command, afraid of what he had planned.

Holloway wrapped one hand around her throat and lifted the glass of water to her lips. "I want to feel you swallow my gift."

The sexual undertone of the act was unsettling, but the need for water proved too great and she eagerly swallowed.

He pressed his hand harder against her throat and groaned in pleasure as she swallowed the life-giving water.

"Slow down," he ordered her. "I want to savor this moment."

Despite her revulsion, Brie took slower sips to the lurid sounds of him groaning in pleasure.

Once Brie had finished half of the glass, he put it back on the nightstand and picked up a bite-sized piece of watermelon. She immediately opened her mouth and held back a moan when he placed it in her mouth and she bit into the succulent fruit. The sweet flavor of the watermelon burst in her mouth and gave her much-needed hydration and calories.

"Swallow," he commanded.

When she did, his voice caught as he groaned even more loudly.

Brie shuddered in disgust.

"I feel you trembling," he stated lustfully. "I always knew you were meant for this." He took his time, telling her, "Every time you swallow, you are purposely bringing me pleasure."

The thought of it nauseated Brie. It shocked her how blind Holloway was to her revulsion toward him. However, she knew it would benefit her if he believed he was breaking her down.

Once the fruit was gone, Holloway kept his hand around her neck and tightened his grip. Brie made no move to stop him even when little pinpoints of light blurred her vision, warning her that her she was about to pass out.

To her relief, he let go and she immediately collapsed to the floor, pretending to cough uncontrollably.

"Can't handle a little breath play, songbird?" he laughed arrogantly. "We'll need to work on that."

Still coughing, Brie curled up into a ball on the floor, wanting to appear weaker than she was.

"I'm setting up a special surprise for you." Holloway

held out his hand to her. "But first, you must be properly prepared."

Brie shuddered when she took his hand and he pulled her up to her feet. She was certain he was planning a new form of punishment.

For Holloway, this was just an elaborate game. She and Mary were simply pawns to be played with because they'd dared to defy him.

The lack of food and water, the cold temperatures, along with her confinement in the dark, were wearing her down. Brie wasn't sure how much longer she could fight.

There was no inkling of humanity left in the man to appeal to. The only way she could survive was to make him believe he was breaking her down, but the horrible truth was…

It was beginning to work.

Holloway led her to the chains attached to the wall. "I'll need you in the right frame of mind for your next surprise."

Brie kept her head lowered and did not resist when he grabbed her wrist, but she whimpered involuntarily when she felt the cold metal against her skin as he secured the cuff and locked it in place. Holloway chuckled in amusement, enjoying her response as he took her other wrist and did the same.

Fisting her hair, he lifted her head to look her in the eyes. "Tomorrow will complete your training, songbird."

When he released his hold, she let her head drop back down.

He opened the door before turning off the lamp.

Laughing on his way out, he added ominously, "You may not survive it."

The instant the door closed, she was enshrouded in darkness again. Brie could already feel the strain of this new position and knew sleep would be impossible.

But...

She could also feel the burst of energy from the food she'd consumed. She understood she must conserve it at all costs. Sir's command for her to wait felt like a solemn promise.

Brie only needed to hold out a little longer because Sir was coming to save her.

Not only did her arms, back, and legs ache from being chained to the wall, but her thirst had returned with a vengeance. Brie had to focus on her breathing to survive the unbearable agony.

As she stood there, her thoughts began to drift in and out of reality. There was a point where she swore that Hope and Anthony were playing on the floor in front of her. Hope was building a tall structure out of colorful blocks while Anthony lay on a blanket, watching his big sister.

When the blocks tumbled down and Brie heard Hope's infectious laughter, she smiled.

Anthony lay on his back and tried to grab a block that had landed near him. Determined to get it, he lifted his legs and rolled to one side. Balling both hands into fists, he powered through, grinning as he successfully rolled onto his stomach.

Brie watched with tears in her eyes as he grasped the block and brought it to his mouth to chew on. "You did it, Antony!" she cried out.

As soon as she spoke, her children vanished, and she was smothered in blackness again. Brie choked back the emotional loss, the ache in her heart suddenly eclipsing her physical pain.

She missed her children on a level she couldn't endure. The thought of never seeing her babies again tore at her heart, stirring something primal and dangerous inside of her.

Brie stared into the darkness and vowed that whatever Holloway had planned today, she would survive it for the sake of her children.

Nothing could keep her from them!

With her resolve renewed, she waited in the dark for Holloway.

However, it was not Holloway who entered the room. Instead, Venom came for her. Goosebumps rose on her skin as he unbound her from the chains. She could not mask the instinctual fear she had of him.

He watched with indifference as she collapsed to the floor. The disdain he felt for her was palpable. "Get up. It's time to meet your maker."

She felt like a prisoner being led to her own execution.

No! Brie would not allow his words to worm their way into her heart.

This man knew how to incite fear because he fed off

it. But she would not let him steal her power. Struggling to her feet, she took a deep breath, drawing her strength.

This is not the end.

With more courage than she knew she possessed, Brie held up her head and walked out of the room to face the dark unknown.

Venom said nothing as he took her to visit the twins again.

Although she was angry at the girls for snitching on her, Brie understood why they'd done it. She suspected there were hidden cameras documenting their every move. If the girls hadn't reported that she had spoken to them multiple times, Mary would still have been punished.

However, the twins would also have paid the price. The only way to survive in this environment was to obey.

Knowing that, Brie kept silent and lowered her head the entire time they meticulously cleaned her body. She was determined not to be the reason anyone was punished today.

Unlike before, the twins took considerable time styling her hair and applying makeup. She was not given a garment to wear. Instead, they left her naked but placed a strange collar around her neck.

The collar was blood-red and covered in black lettering Brie couldn't read. The weight of it around her throat filled Brie with a sense of foreboding.

When the twins presented her to Venom, the girl held up her fist to indicate zero infractions. Venom glanced at Brie with disappointment, roughly pushing her forward.

She shivered, realizing the man was upset that he would not get to punish Mary further.

Brie faced the stairs, her scalp tingling as an overwhelming sense of dread coursed through her.

She couldn't move.

She made a silent, fervent cry to Sir, begging him to rescue her.

Her bottom lip trembled as Venom forced her up the stairs and she silently made a promise to herself.

No matter what happens, I will not break. Holloway will never own my soul.

When Brie reached the top of the stairs, she was surprised to see the place was empty of people. But it was far from silent.

A violent storm swirled outside. The whole place echoed with the sound of the large raindrops pelting the glass panes. The lightning hit so close that the thunder shook the windows.

Brie's heart dropped because it dashed any hope of rescue.

Venom shoved her forward, leading her to the large room. When they entered, Brie instantly noticed Mary wore the same blood-red collar that she wore.

Mary was tied to a chair in the center of the room. Her hands were bound behind her back and her ankles secured tightly to the legs of the chair.

Mary's chin rested on her chest, her whole body radiating defeat. Brie had never seen anything more terrifying.

Glancing around the room, Brie noticed numerous film cameras stationed strategically to catch various angles, all pointing to the center of the room.

When she heard Holloway's voice, she turned to see him speaking to five men dressed in expensive suits. They were seated comfortably in a row of overstuffed leather chairs.

Holloway smiled when he saw her. Brie didn't miss the malicious glint in his eye when he stated, "Now, for an evening we will not forget."

The five men nodded. All of them looked hungrily at Brie's naked body as though they were predators ready for a feast.

Holloway folded his arms and asked with a cruel smile, "Songbird, are you ready to become famous?"

Brie looked back at Mary in fear, wanting to call out to her. But she remained silent, knowing Mary would be punished for it.

"Gentlemen, I am familiar with your particular tastes and have brought two slaves for your entertainment. There are no limits to tonight's play. If either one of the slaves refuses, the other will die."

Brie gasped in horror.

The sound of the five men's obscene laughter would forever be burned in her heart.

"As host, I shall begin the evening with some harmless fun," Holloway informed them.

Brie swallowed hard as she watched Holloway approach Mary while still addressing the men. "You all know this one is my prized possession. I've groomed her since she was a child to take the place of her whore of a mother."

He lifted Mary's chin and looked down at her beautiful face. Mary kept her gaze lowered while he spoke. "She is nearly perfect, but she has a rebellious streak that has yet to be eradicated. I plan to cure her of that tonight…one way or another."

The men's malicious laughter continued.

These people have no souls!

"You may not be aware of this, but she is an expert at fellatio. Better than any hooker I've ever had."

The men grunted their approval.

Without warning, Holloway slapped Mary's face with the same power behind it that he'd used on Brie at the theatre. The sound of the impact echoed through the room.

Brie immediately closed her eyes and retreated to her dream in the wildflower field. However, she couldn't block out the horrible sound of him slapping Mary's face while he verbally humiliated her in front of those men.

Brie had to force back the tears when it occurred to her that what he was doing was eerily similar to the abuse Mary suffered at the hands of her stepfather. She knew it was a calculated tactic on Holloway's part.

He wanted to trigger Mary before the night even began!

The room suddenly lit up as lightning flashed nearby. Brie opened her eyes just as the thunder followed, making the windows rattle violently.

Unfazed by the storm raging outside, Holloway

barked, "Look at me!"

She saw Mary obediently lift her head to meet his gaze. However, Mary did not disguise the hatred she felt as she glared up at him.

Holloway smiled, slapping her face again. "Ah, that rebellious streak raises its ugly head again. It will make tonight far more entertaining!"

Based on the erections straining their expensive pants, Brie could tell the men who were watching were turned on by the violence. However, they were not like the audience from the other night. These men were not playing with themselves like teenage boys. No, they were actively observing the scene with a detached excitement that felt inhuman.

Before leaving Mary's side, Holloway slapped her face with such force that her neck snapped backward. Still, Mary remained silent, not giving him the satisfaction of her cries.

Brie held her breath when Holloway turned his gaze on her. "We're off to a promising start but now it's your turn, songbird."

She prayed for strength as Holloway approached her, his eyes gleaming with predatory excitement.

Turning to face the men, he asked, "Isaac, would you like the honor of being next?"

An older man with a long gray beard and a robust frame stood up and straightened his jacket before approaching Brie.

He walked around her, studying her body like it was a piece of meat. "The skin is pristine," he complimented Holloway.

"I was mindful of that during training," Holloway replied. "An admirer of your work, I wanted you to have an untouched canvas."

The man snorted in appreciation.

The aura the man radiated was one of pure brutality. Brie's skin crawled just being near him. When he reached out to touch her, Brie instinctively shied away.

"Uh-uh-uh…" Holloway warned her, then glanced back at Mary.

Closing her eyes, Brie endured the man's touch as he ran his hands over her breasts and belly. "I see she's had children," he stated with disappointment.

"Two, to be exact. It makes her a perfect candidate for tonight's entertainment. Her mothering instincts will play well into this challenge."

The man's hands became more aggressive as he explored her body, looking for sensitive areas that were susceptible to pain. "Does she like the cane?"

Brie involuntarily shuddered.

Although Marquis Gray had once shown her the tool could be used for pleasure, she knew the extreme pain it could produce.

Chuckling, the man told Holloway, "I enjoyed seeing her reaction when I mentioned the cane."

"This slave is not a masochist," Holloway proudly informed him.

"Good." The man cupped her chin and lifted it to study her face, murmuring, "I find that *very* arousing."

"I look forward to hearing my songbird sing for you tonight."

Holloway snapped his fingers and Venom left, re-

turning with a rolling cart covered in a wide variety of dangerous instruments. Along with a cruel-looking cane, Brie's eyes were drawn to the sharpened hooks and a vicious flogger made of barbed wire. Numb with fear, she stared down at all the instruments on the cart. She knew with certainty that every tool on display would be used on them tonight.

Thunder rocked the building again as the chaotic storm ramped up.

Closing her eyes, Brie stilled her thoughts. She would not let fear steal away the strength she needed to meet this trial.

When she opened her eyes again, she caught a glimpse of a shadowy figure outlined by a lightning flash just outside the window. Her heart raced as she fought to remain calm.

The old man picked up the cane, stroking it lovingly. "This is a Tohiti." He whipped it around, cutting the air with its ferocity. "They are commonly used in prisons."

With a gleam in his eye, he added, "It is quite heavy and causes extreme pain when applied correctly." He grazed his hand over her bare skin. "What I like most are the permanent marks my cane leaves behind."

The other men grunted like animals and shifted in their seats, turned on by the promise of violence.

No longer afraid, Brie met the man's unholy gaze.

Lightning flashed above with thunder immediately following. It was so close that the entire building shook from its force.

Sir was here…

Her Protector

"Bind her arms above her head and gag her," the bearded man commanded. "I don't want to be distracted from my art."

Brie could feel the man's intense level of sexual arousal as he gripped his cane tightly. Meanwhile, Venom gagged her and secured her wrists to a chain, pulling it taut above her head.

Brie kept her eyes set forward and blinked slowly as if she were meekly accepting her fate, not wanting to not give away her desire to catch another glimpse of Sir.

Holloway's eyes shone with an ungodly light as he waited for the macabre scene to begin while the storm raged outside.

Brie shuddered in disgust when the old man ran his hands over her bare skin. He looked into the nearest camera and smiled. "And now for my newest creation."

Glancing in Mary's direction, Brie found her friend staring at her. The devastating hopelessness on Mary's face made Brie's heart clench up in a way she'd never felt

before. It was as if she could feel Mary's despair to the depths of her soul.

Brie fixed her gaze forward again. Her heart raced as the old man positioned himself in front of her and stared at her breasts, a lurid smile curling his lips.

When he lifted the cane, Brie was blinded by a brilliant flash as lightning struck the building. The lights flickered, and the crack of thunder that followed was absolutely terrifying.

"God, this is going to make for a great film!" Holloway cried out excitedly, rubbing his hands together.

Momentarily shaken by the ferocity of the storm, her tormentor focused on Brie again. He raised his arm to deliver the first agonizing stroke of the cane.

Brie squeezed her eyes shut, anticipating the explosion of pain to follow. When it failed to come, she opened them to see Sir wrestling the cane from the man's hand.

Unable to move or speak, Brie hung there helplessly bound in the chains, watching as a legion of men led by Captain subdued Holloway, Venom, and the other four men in a matter of seconds.

Master Anderson, Baron, and Titov came to assist Sir. Two of them grabbed the old man's arms, pinioning them behind his back, while Master Anderson drove his knee into the man's back, pushing him to the floor. Once they had immobilized her tormentor, Sir rushed to Brie and freed her from the chains before ripping the gag from her mouth.

Enveloping her in his powerful embrace, he held her tightly.

"You're safe, babygirl."

Brie was mute with shock, unable to believe he was really there in the flesh, worried it was another dream or a hallucination.

She heard Captain cry out plaintively, "Leif!"

Brie watched, with her face pressed against Sir's chest, as Captain raced to Mary. He pulled a knife from his belt and made quick work of the ropes, gathering Mary into his arms. A profound relief flooded Brie knowing they were both safe.

Holloway couldn't hurt them anymore.

Brie began shaking uncontrollably as her body reacted to the shock of everything that had happened. Sir pulled away, looking at her with concern.

She broke down sobbing. Wrapping her arms tighter around him, Brie buried her face in his chest, determined to never let go of him.

Safe…

"Do you need a medic?" Sir asked her.

Brie could hear the agony in his voice but shook her head against his chest, not wanting to break their embrace. Holding her tight with one arm, Sir undid the horrid blood-red collar around her neck and threw it across the room. He then took the blanket he was handed and wrapped it around her.

Pulling the phone from his pocket, Sir told Brie, "There are three phone calls we must make."

Brie closed her eyes, soaking in his strength as she listened to him dial and then speak into the phone. "She's safe. I have her in my arms right now."

Her ears perked up when she heard Rytsar's voice on

the other end. She was surprised he wasn't here.

"Yes, I'm certain she wants to talk to you," Sir stated, handing Brie his phone.

"Rytsar," she whimpered.

"Are you okay, *radost moya*?"

She took a moment to answer. "I will be…"

Brie heard his voice break when he told her, "I have not been able to sleep since the day you were taken."

Her bottom lip trembled. "I channeled your strength when you were caged in Siberia."

She heard him start to cry. "I'm grateful…you are alive, *radost moya.*"

Brie looked up at Sir. He gave her a reassuring smile, but she could see he was struggling to keep his emotions in check.

"I'm safe, Rytsar," she assured him.

Rytsar let out a tortured groan. "I would give anything to be with you right now."

Brie frowned, clutching the phone. "Why aren't you here?"

"I cannot leave Russia, but I sent Titov in my stead."

"Durov will explain later, babygirl" Sir interrupted. "We have two more calls to make."

"I have to go," Brie told Rytsar with regret. "I want you to know I love you."

"My love for you is immense, *radost moya,* and I thank the God Almighty my prayers have been answered."

Sir took the phone from her to dial another number. "She's safe. I know you want to hear her voice so I am passing the phone to her."

Brie took it, looking at him questioningly.

He mouthed the words, *Your parents.*

Brie nodded, her voice catching when she said, "Mama…"

"Oh, my God, you're safe!" her mother cried.

"Is that Brianna?" she heard her father shout in the background.

"It is, it is!" her mother answered. "They found her, Bill!"

She immediately asked Brie, "Please tell me you're all right."

"I am, Mama," she answered. "Sir saved me."

"Thank the Lord!" her father replied. "We've been worried sick about you, little girl."

"I never gave up hope, Daddy."

Brie looked at Sir gratefully.

"I can't believe it, I'm just so grateful," her mother sniffled through her tears. "It's wonderful to hear your voice, sweetheart."

Brie thought she heard her daughter in the background and asked, "Is Hope there with you?"

"Yes!" her mother replied. "We've been watching the children while Thane searched for you."

Brie's voice trembled with joy when she asked, "Can I talk to her?"

"Of course, little girl," her father answered. She heard him grunt as he lifted Hope up.

"Hey, sweet pea. It's Mommy."

"Mama."

Brie swallowed back the painful lump in her throat when she heard her daughter's beautiful voice.

"I love you, sweet pea!" she cried, barely able to

choke out the words.

Hearing her cry, Hope whimpered, "Mama?"

Brie held back her emotions, swallowing several times before she said in a sing-song voice, "Mommy is coming home. I can't wait to see you and Antony so I can give you both a great big hug."

Giggling, her mother told Brie, "I know you can't see this, but Hope is pointing at Antony right now. She has the biggest smile on her face."

Brie knew she was about to break down in happy tears which would only confuse Hope, so she told her, "Sweet pea, can you give Antony a big kiss for Mommy?"

To her parents, she said, "I've got to go, but I want you to know how much I love you both."

"We love you too, dear heart!"

"I'm not going to believe you're safe until I see you with my own eyes," her father stated, his voice strained with emotion.

"I'll be home soon, Daddy."

Brie's hands were shaking, her heart bursting with joy, when she gave Sir back the phone. "Thank you. I needed to hear their voices."

Sir squeezed her tightly. "Your parents have been out of their minds with worry but have done a phenomenal job making sure our children are cared for."

Sir dialed the last number and immediately stated, "Brie's safe."

He then handed her the phone as he explained, "I promised I would call him when I found you. I don't think we would have located you in time without his guidance."

Brie frowned, wondering who it was when she put the phone up to her ear. "Hello?"

Tono's warm voice filled the air. "Toriko."

His voice was like a warm blanket to her soul. "Oh, Tono…"

"I *knew* Sir Davis would find you."

"He did," she said, hugging Sir in gratitude.

Tono paused for a moment before stated sadly, "You have suffered much, toriko."

Brie nodded as tears started to fall. "Sir says you helped to find me."

"The connection you and I have is still strong."

Clutching the phone tighter, she confessed, "There were times when breathing was my only escape."

"I know," he said solemnly.

Brie's heart skipped a beat. She wondered if the connection she had felt hadn't been as one-sided as she'd thought. Before she could ask Tono, she caught a whiff of smoke.

Goosebumps suddenly rose on her skin. "Something's wrong!" she cried out. "We have to get them out now!"

"Who?" Sir asked, taking the phone from her.

"There are other people locked in the basement!"

"How many, Brianna?" Captain demanded, walking up to them.

Brie shook her head. "I don't know. At least fourteen that I've seen, but there could be more." She turned to Sir, crying in desperation, "We have to save them!"

Sir turned to Captain. "The lightning must have

sparked a fire. We need to get everyone out immediately."

Captain became all business, telling one of his men, "Alert the medic team that there are more coming." Pointing to a small group, he ordered, "See if you can locate the fire and put it out."

To the rest under his command, he shouted, "Head downstairs. It appears we have a minimum of fourteen captives locked in the basement."

"Yes, Captain," they answered in unison.

Motioning to Master Anderson, Baron, Titov, and Sir, he stated, "We have no time to lose."

Sir turned to Brie. "Head outside with Mary."

"No!" Mary staggered toward the group, tightly clutching the blanket around her. "I'm going with you. I know where they are."

Captain frowned. "But you are weak, leif."

She looked him dead in the eye. "I'm *not* leaving them behind."

"Me, either!" Brie agreed.

Sir gripped Brie's shoulders. "I will not risk losing you again. Go outside and wait for me there."

"But I have to help save them!" Brie told him.

Sir shook her. "I'm adamant about this, Brie. I will help rescue them, but *you* must go to the waiting vehicles outside. Promise me."

"There's no time to lose!" Captain shouted, as he roughly patted down Holloway and found the set of keys on him. He headed toward the stairs with Mary right beside him.

Obeying Sir, Brie headed in the opposite direction

and noticed several of Captain's men dragging Venom to one of the vans. She called out to them, "Wait!"

After a quick search, Brie found his set of keys. She headed back inside, startled to find it already filling up with smoke.

Brie understood that Sir wanted to protect her, but she knew the keys were vital to getting everyone out alive—promise or no promise.

Inferno

Brie headed down the stairwell with the keys jingling in her hand. She shivered in fear when she reached the bottom stair. This place held so much horror and pain that she was desperate to find someone to hand the keys to so she could leave.

She was disheartened to see the light haze of smoke in the basement because it meant there was very little time left…

Hearing voices to her right, Brie headed in that direction but took a wrong turn and ended up at a dead end. She retraced her steps but soon found herself at another dead end.

"Where are you?" she yelled, heading down another hallway.

Brie stopped in her tracks when she heard muffled cries coming from the row of doors ahead. When she tried to open the nearest door, she found it locked. Fumbling through the different keys, she eventually found the correct one but was frustrated when she found the room empty.

"Hello! Can you hear me?" she called out. Unable to pinpoint which door led to the room where the voices were coming from, Brie started frantically unlocking every single door while the hallway began to fill up with smoke.

Panic set in when she dropped the keys. Not willing to run, Brie cried, "Shout as loud as you can until I find you."

She closed her eyes and remained still, straining to hear their voices. Certain the muffled cries were coming from the right side, Brie began unlocking that row of doors. She had to blink away the tears from the stinging smoke, concentrating hard to slide the key into the lock.

Opening another door, Brie saw the twins frantically straining against their chains. They'd been gagged and bound on opposite walls. Closing the door behind her to keep the smoke out, Brie raced to the nearest one and tried every key until she managed to unlock the metal cuffs.

Brie hurried to the other twin once the girl was free. After removing their gags, Brie explained, "The building is on fire, but I have no idea how to get out of here."

"We do," they both answered.

The nearest twin grabbed Brie's hand while the other opened the door. As they started down the smoke-filled hallway, Brie noticed fresh wounds on the girls' naked bodies.

"Are there any others in this hallway?" she cried.

"No, our Lord keeps us separate from the others."

Turning a corner, they ran into a group of rescuers.

Brie heard Sir's stern voice. "What the hell are you doing. Brie? You're not supposed to be here!"

Brie held out the keys to him with a shaking hand. "I brought more keys so you could rescue them faster."

Sir snatched the keys from her and barked to the twins, "Get her out of here. Now!"

The twins each took a hand and raced Brie down the hallway toward safety. Glancing back, Brie was frightened to see Sir heading in the opposite direction.

"Come with me!" she begged.

He turned and commanded, "Wait for me outside."

Brie whimpered, terrified she might never see him again as the twins continued to propel her forward.

"I love you, Brianna," he called out.

Everything in her wanted to break away and turn back, but she'd made Sir a promise she could not break. "Come back to me!" she cried as she lost sight of him in the haze.

By the time they made it outside, all three of them were choking on the smoke. Titov quickly guided the three to a triage area where the team of medics was waiting for them.

While the medical staff administered her oxygen and gave her more blankets, Brie stared in horror watching the entire back of the building engulfed in flames. Her gaze was drawn to the entrance of the building as she desperately waited for Sir to appear.

Wrapped in warm blankets, she watched as group after group of Captain's men emerged from the billowing smoke, leading survivors to safety.

Brie closed her eyes, silently praying that Sir would

be the next person to walk out.

When she opened them again, she screamed in sheer terror as a portion of the roof collapsed. Bolting to her feet, she attempted to run back inside, but Titov grabbed her and forced her to sit back down.

"You're not going anywhere. Rytsar's orders."

"Where's Captain?" Brie asked him, scanning the crowd of people. She was certain he would know where Sir was.

"He hasn't returned yet."

Brie frowned. "Have you seen Mary?"

"*Nyet*, Mrs. Davis."

Brie stood up again. "I can't just sit here and do nothing!"

"But you will," Titov insisted, pushing her back down.

"I can't lose them all…" Brie whimpered. A feeling of helplessness washed over her as she stared at the entrance billowing with smoke.

Titov assured her, "I've worked with Captain before. He will not jeopardize his team."

While Brie knew in her heart that what Titov said was true, it didn't quell her growing fear as she watched the fire burn even brighter.

Brie's heart leapt with joy when Mary finally emerged, leading four young women out. All five were struggling to breathe after inhaling the thick smoke. They were immediately led to the triage station.

"Mary, where's Sir?" Brie shouted from where she sat.

Mary pointed back toward the building.

Brie frowned, panic setting in. Several minutes later, Captain walked out with Master Anderson and Baron who were leading nine more people to safety.

Captain stated proudly to everyone assembled, "We've got them all."

Brie held her breath as she waited for Sir to emerge at the tail end of the group. When he didn't show, she slipped out of Titov's grasp and ran headlong toward Captain, screaming, "Where's Thane? Where's my husband?"

Shaking his head, Captain wiped the soot from his face. "I thought he made it out before me."

Master Anderson immediately volunteered to re-enter the burning building. Brie whimpered when Captain answered, "No! It's not safe."

Instead, Captain headed back to the entrance himself to find Sir.

Brie cried out in relief when Sir suddenly emerged from the dark smoke, bare-chested, using his shirt to cover the face of a tiny baby cradled in his arms.

"Thane!" Brie sobbed, racing to him.

He handed the infant to a medic but refused care for himself. Pulling Brie into his arms, he told her, "I couldn't leave once I heard a child was missing."

She looked up at him through her tears. "I'm just grateful you're safe…"

The medic caring for the baby asked, "Where's the mother?"

Sir looked sadly at the baby, "I was told she passed away several days ago."

Brie glanced at the dark van that housed the man

responsible for this evil and raged, "May he rot in hell forever!"

Looking back at the building, Brie watched with satisfaction as the flames consumed it. It was fitting that this hellish place should be consumed by fire.

However, it was surreal how the inferno continued to grow while the rain drenched the forest around it. It felt as if God Himself wanted to rid the world of the evil bound up in this place.

Sir kept his arm tightly wrapped around Brie as they watched the entire building collapse, the fire gutting it from the inside out.

Mary walked up to them but avoided eye contact with Brie when she asked the medic, "Will the baby be okay?"

"His vitals are stable, but he is severely underweight. With proper care, however, he should recover."

Mary picked up the tiny baby. Looking down at the infant, her voice caught when she said, "You didn't deserve this..."

Captain came over to speak to Sir. "The local authorities have been contacted and are on their way."

Sir looked in satisfaction at the numerous survivors. "Excellent work, Captain. I'll call Stephanie to see if she can house all of them."

"Good."

Sir held out his hand to Captain and shook it firmly. "This rescue would not have been possible without you."

Captain nodded gravely. "I'm thankful we were able to save them all." He glanced at Mary and Brie with a troubled expression. "However, I wish we'd gotten here sooner to spare them any pain."

Sir cleared his throat. "As do I."

Brie watched as the police arrived, lighting up the forest with flashing red and blue lights. She held her breath as Greg Holloway was taken out of the van in handcuffs and led to a waiting patrol car.

Holloway's reign of terror was over.

Brie attempted to speak to Mary while they were at the hospital being evaluated, but her friend kept her eyes on the floor and completely ignored Brie.

While it was hurtful, she had witnessed firsthand the pain Mary endured because of her. The wounds on Mary's back had yet to heal and would leave scars she would have to live with for a lifetime.

As much as Brie longed to comfort Mary, she respected her friend's need for distance. Brie hoped there would come a day when Mary could find it in her heart to forgive her.

Brie lay on the hospital gurney in Emergency for a long time while they administered several IVs. As she watched the liquid slowly drip into her veins, she heard Captain walk in and ask the station nurse if he could speak to Mary.

He was directed to the curtained area right next to Brie. "I will take you home, lief. Is there anything I can get you before the long drive?"

She heard Mary's tortured voice answer, "No…"

"Candy and I would like you to remain with us. Would you like that?"

Mary said nothing.

"If you'd rather stay somewhere else, I will arrange it."

She started weeping. "I just want…"

"Yes?" Captain encouraged her softly.

"…to forget," she said, sobbing quietly.

Captain told her in a tender voice, "If I could, I would take those memories from you, lief. But I can't. What I can do is help you move past them…with time."

"I want to shrivel up and die," she choked out.

"I understand," he replied. "There was a time when I felt that way, myself."

"What saved you?" Mary asked, weeping softly.

"A three-legged dog I didn't want."

She was silent for a moment. "That's the last answer I expected."

Chuckling sadly, he told her, "I felt the same at the time, but you never know the gifts life has in store for you. The only way to experience them is to keep on fighting."

"I'm tired of fighting, Vader…"

Captain stated softly, "Let me be your three-legged dog for a while."

Tears filled Brie's eyes as she lay there, touched by Captain's kind heart. For a man renowned for his tough exterior and military know-how, he was truly a gentle giant inside.

Unlikely Ally

Finishing up the hospital paperwork so she could return home, Brie heard a shy voice behind her say, "Thank you."

Brie turned and was surprised to see the twins standing there, their wounds freshly bandaged. The two were holding tightly to each other's hands.

She smiled. "I'm glad to see you're both okay."

One of the girls pointed to herself and said timidly, "My name is Mia."

Brie nodded. "I'm Brianna, but most people call me Brie."

The girl squeezed her sister's hand harder. Looking at Brie with deep regret, she said, "When you walked into our cell today, I was terrified."

Brie frowned in shock. "Why?"

"I could smell the smoke and was afraid my sister and I would burn to death in that dungeon. I can't tell you the joy I felt when the door opened. But the moment I saw it was you, I was certain you would leave us to our fate."

Brie shook her head, not understanding.

The other twin spoke up. "It's because of me. The terrible thing I did...telling on you."

When Brie reached out to comfort the girl, she flinched in response. Lowering her hand, Brie assured her, "I don't hold it against you. You probably would have been punished if you hadn't." She looked at the young woman with sympathy. "What happened to me wasn't your fault. *None* of it was your fault."

The girl stared at Brie with tortured eyes. "You promised my sister and me that rescue was coming, but I didn't believe you." Her bottom lip trembled. "You were so brave, while I...acted like a coward."

Brie felt compassion for her. "You did what you needed to do to survive. No one can fault you for that."

"But I regret doing it," she confessed tearfully.

Brie was instantly taken back to Mary's terrible punishment, the whole grotesque scene suddenly playing out again in her head. She jumped, her dark thoughts mercifully interrupted, when Sir came up to her and announced, "It's time for us to leave, babygirl."

The twins instantly bowed their heads and began shaking. They squeezed each other's hands so tightly that their knuckles were white.

Sir instantly noticed their discomfort and took several steps back from the two girls.

"Ladies, you will be driven to the Tatianna Legacy Center," he informed them. "The woman who runs it is named Stephanie. She is a survivor herself and will take excellent care of you."

They nodded but kept their heads bowed low.

Brie despised Holloway even more after seeing these women's instinctual response to Sir, because of what they'd endured. It would take countless years for them to recover from the trauma.

Sir held out his arm to Brie, looking at the twins in concern. "Can I can get you both anything before we leave the hospital?"

The twins said nothing, shaking even more noticeably. Understanding his presence was only causing them distress, Sir quickly escorted Brie out to the vehicle waiting for them.

A police officer walked up to Sir and nodded at Brie. "I need to ask her some questions before you leave."

"Mrs. Davis will provide a written statement," Sir informed him curtly. "Right now, I'm taking my wife home."

Sir helped Brie into the vehicle without another word to the man. Once he joined her inside, Sir slammed the car door shut and told the driver to head out.

Looking at her gently, Sir patted his lap. "Come here, babygirl."

Brie closed her eyes and laid her head on his lap. She sighed gratefully when he began stroking her hair. Sir had arranged for a private vehicle for the long trip home. He ordered the driver to raise the partition so they could speak freely.

But Brie didn't want to talk.

She longed to simply lay there and forget everything that happened. However, she felt a growing uneasiness that even Sir's touch could not erase.

Sir was patient, petting her hair for several hours, but that feeling of uneasiness had only increased over time and was starting to frighten her.

Sitting up, she faced him. She knew Sir was holding back his questions and decided to tell him everything in the hopes that talking about it would release the growing apprehension she felt.

"I need to talk."

Sir nodded. "I'm listening."

Brie decided not to hold anything back. If the roles were reversed, she would want him to do the same because not knowing every detail would be torture for her.

Letting out an anxious sigh, Brie started from the very beginning, starting with what happened as soon as she arrived at the Egyptian.

Sir caressed her cheek, looking grief-stricken when he told her, "I remember feeling a check in my spirit. It was like ice running through my veins. When I tried to call you and you didn't answer, I completely lost it." He stared at Brie as if he was seeing a ghost—as if he couldn't believe she was really there beside him.

Brie could feel his tension mounting when he shared, "I cannot express the level of fear that gripped me at that moment. Knowing that you needed me, but not knowing where you were was terrifying."

Brie looked into his troubled eyes, wishing she could wash away the terror he'd felt. Shaking her head, she admitted, "I can't tell you how much I regretted not texting the name of the theatre, but by some miracle you still found us." She looked at him in wonder. "Holloway broke my phone as soon as he kidnapped me. How were you able to track it?"

"He's an old fool. I only needed its last known location. The moment I saw you were at The Egyptian I knew with certainty that Holloway was involved. I immediately called the police and got in my car, driving like a bat out of hell to save you."

Sir looked bereft when he confessed, "I don't know how the hell Holloway was able to escape when our response was so quick…"

His voice trailed off as he shook his head in painful disbelief. "It was as if I was living Rytsar's nightmare with Tatianna. I know exactly how he felt when I found out we'd missed you by mere minutes…"

Brie could feel the weight of his suffering and placed her hand over his heart. "But I heard the sirens. It gave me strength to know help was coming."

He pulled her into his embrace. "It tears me apart that I didn't save you when we were so close…"

Brie clung to Sir, wanting him to know the difference he made. "The moment Holloway heard the sirens, he was forced to abandon the punishment he planned."

"What punishment?" Sir growled.

Brie pulled back, unable to look him in the eye. "He brought three men with him to punish me."

"What did they do to you?" Sir asked, rage boiling under his breath.

"Nothing," she assured him. "Because the minute they heard the sirens, they ran."

"At least I spared you from that…" Sir said gruffly, then his eyes darkened. "But I failed to save you from

Holloway."

Brie closed her eyes, remembering the terror she'd felt when she was captured.

"There was blood at the theatre," Sir stated. "We found Holloway's blood, linking him to the scene."

Brie opened her eyes, nodding. "I bit his hand trying to get away. It only enraged him more, but I'm thankful it helped."

"How the hell did he avoid the police?" Sir asked her.

Brie explained how the two of them escaped through the tunnels between the theatres.

Sir shook his head in disbelief. "Why didn't you run?"

"Holloway threatened to kill Mary if I escaped." Although Brie had suffered greatly for that decision, she did not regret it. "He would have, Sir."

"Yes," he agreed somberly.

Brie met Sir's gaze but couldn't stop her bottom lip from trembling. "I began to lose hope once we arrived at the compound and I realized how isolated we were." Looking at him questioningly, she asked, "How did you find us, Sir?"

He let out a ragged sigh. "The tip came from such an unlikely source that I questioned its validity. To be honest, I was certain it was a trap, but with nothing else to go on, I had no other choice but to take it at face value."

Sir kissed her tenderly on the forehead. "I would have done anything to save you at that point, babygirl. Even if it meant walking into a trap that would have ended in my death."

Brie placed her trembling hands on his beloved face. Her voice quavered when she choked out, "I'm eternally grateful it didn't come to that."

He stared into her eyes, before crushing her hard against his chest. "I never thought in a million years that Darius would be the one to help save you."

Brie pulled away, shaking her head violently. "He was there, Sir! He took pleasure in what Holloway was doing. Darius is just as evil as he is!"

With a pained expression, Sir said, "He admitted that he had partnered with Holloway to further his career. But Darius claimed when he was invited to join Holloway at his exclusive BDSM party, he'd had no idea you would be there."

Sir then let out a low, ominous growl. "When I demanded he tell me what happened at that party, Darius refused to say. However, he insisted you were not harmed."

"I may not have been touched, but I was definitely *harmed* by what happened!" Brie cried.

Sir stiffened, his voice hoarse with regret when he told her, "I wish I had gotten there in time to prevent it."

Knowing he was riddled with guilt, Brie looked deep into his eyes. "I knew you would rescue us. That's what gave me the strength to keep fighting every day."

"You should never have been forced to endure Holloway's perversity!" he growled.

Brie felt the heaviness of his remorse and reminded him, "I'm *here* because of you."

"Not just me, babygirl. Rytsar sent all the men he

could spare. Anderson and Baron stepped up, and Captain volunteered to lead us all in the search."

Sir took her hand in his and squeezed it. His voice was full of agony when he asked, "What did you endure, Brie? I need to know."

She knew the time had come. As an act of love for him and a need for healing, Brie allowed the memories to flood back in as she detailed the torturous experiences she'd suffered at the hands of Holloway.

Sir kept silent, gritting his teeth while she shared the details of the horrific days leading up to the rescue.

Rage burned in Sir's eyes when he told her, "Deprivation of sleep, water, food, and light, along with the loud music and being forced to watch Mary's torture…all of those are the same techniques governments around the world use to psychologically break prisoners without leaving a mark."

Shuddering, she asked, "How long has it been? I don't even know…"

"Eight days," he answered, adding in a strained voice, "Eight days too long."

Brie looked at him in shock. "Eight days? It felt like weeks." She shook her head. "I can't believe it…eight days?"

"Babygirl, hardened criminals suffering such torture have broken under less." Sir cupped her cheek. "How did you survive it?"

Tears rolled down her cheeks, when she answered, "I thought of you and our children. But, when even that wasn't enough, I focused on my breathing."

Sir nodded thoughtfully. "Nosaka sensed your suffering. When I called and informed him you had been kidnapped by Holloway, he postponed everything so he could meditate twenty-four-seven until you were found."

Brie looked at Sir in surprise, touched by Tono's response.

"I trust Nosaka's connection with you, and I counted on it while we searched," he told her. "I remember asking if he had any impressions about your location the day you were taken, and he mentioned heavy humidity and the smell of an old forest. Later on, it matched Darius's description, which proved vital when he wasn't able to give us the exact location."

"Why couldn't he give you that?" Brie demanded, still distrustful of the man's motives.

"Darius said that everyone invited to the party was taken on a private jet and blindfolded, which made the entire event feel more exclusive and secretive.

"We could find no records of that flight," Sir continued. "However, Darius knew how long they were in the air and gave us descriptions of the interior of the compound. Between Nosaka's impressions and the information Darius gave us, Captain was able to narrow down the location to the forests of northern California. Even though the compound is off the grid, using surveillance drones, he was able to finally pinpoint the location."

Sir's voice was hoarse with emotion, "I was going crazy every day that passed, afraid we'd be too late…" He closed his eyes, taking a deep breath to collect himself. "But, Nosaka assured me that you were still alive."

Brie heard Sir's sharp intake of breath when she told him, "I think I would be dead today if you hadn't come."

"What the hell did we walk into, Brie? What the fuck was Holloway planning to do to you? And why all the cameras?"

"I..." Brie struggled to speak, overcome by the acute terror she'd felt when it was happening to her. Swallowing hard, she could barely get her words out. "Those men were there to sexually torture us, and whoever..."

Brie's throat closed up, making it impossible to speak.

Sir immediately embraced her. "You don't have to continue."

She soaked in the warmth of his embrace, drawing strength from it. She forced herself to talk, needing to say it—needing the release. "If either Mary or I refused, the other one would be murdered in front of us."

Brie felt Sir's whole body stiffen. "Oh, my God." He shuddered in revulsion. "And Holloway was going to film it..."

His voice trailed off as he began to rock Brie in his arms, murmuring words of comfort. But as the reality of what happened began to sink in, Brie could feel his dark rage simmering under the surface.

Although it came from a place of love and a need to protect, Brie also knew it had the potential to destroy them.

Home

"Let me keep stroking your hair, babygirl," Sir said in a comforting tone.

She laid her head back down in his lap and closed her eyes. His soothing touch was exactly what her heart needed after sharing the details of that terrifying moment. The feeling of unease hadn't dissipated, but being with Sir was a balm for her tattered soul.

After so many days without sleep, his gentle touch lulled her into a deep slumber she didn't wake from until Sir shook her lightly and said, "We're almost home."

Hearing the word "home" filled her heart with immense joy. Brie pulled herself up to a sitting position to gaze out the window as they drove down the familiar streets leading to the house.

Brie felt tingles start at the top of her head. Suddenly, she couldn't breathe…

None of this feels real!

"What's wrong, babygirl?"

Her bottom lip quivered when she confessed, "I'm

afraid…" She lowered her head as tears fell to her lap. "I feel like I'm about to wake up and find myself locked in the darkness again."

"No…" Sir assured her, pulling Brie into his embrace. "You saw the building burn to the ground. You don't have to be afraid of ever going back to that place. None of you do."

Brie nodded, grasping hard to the truth of his words.

"Look," Sir said with enthusiasm as he pointed to the ocean. "We're almost there."

She felt a tangible quickening in her spirit at the thought of seeing her children again. She squeezed him tighter. "You brought me out of that hell and returned me safely to our home."

"I would do anything for you, babygirl." For the first time since her rescue, Sir leaned down to kiss her. It was a gentle, tentative kiss.

Brie closed her eyes, savoring the tenderness of his lips. "Thank you," she whispered. "I've missed your lips."

"I've missed every damn thing about you," he stated fervently.

Brie suddenly felt anxious when the driver pulled into their driveway. It felt intensely surreal to be here after constantly dreaming about it, and fear gripped her heart again.

What if it *was* only a dream?

Rather than let her suffer in her state of shock and confusion, Sir took her hand firmly in his and help her out of the car. "You're home," he reassured her.

The moment Sir opened the door to the house, her

mother ran to Brie, crying, "Oh, my God, you're here! My sweet girl is really here!"

Brie suddenly felt skittish, not wanting to be touched, and she stiffened in her mother's embrace. That feeling only worsened when her father walked up and tried to hug her.

He looked hurt when she backed away, muttering, "I'm sorry."

Confused by her feelings, Brie looked at Sir and whimpered, "I don't know what's wrong with me…"

Sir gathered her into his arms, murmuring, "Nothing's wrong, my dear. You just need time."

Her mother looked at Brier strangely, clearly distraught by her reaction. Her father was shocked by it and growled, "What did that bastard do to you?"

Brie was unprepared to answer his question.

Sir attempted to defuse the situation by telling her parents, "Brianna hasn't had a full night of sleep since the day she was kidnapped."

Her mother held her hands up to her mouth, crying "My poor little girl… did the brute even feed you? Let me make you something to eat!" Her mother ran to the kitchen without waiting for her answer.

It was obvious her parents' reaction they had no idea that she had been tortured and almost killed.

Her father stared hard at Brie. "What did Greg Holloway do to you that you would react this way to your own father?"

Brie wasn't willing to tell him and looked desperately at Sir.

Sir immediately took charge of the situation. "Dad,

Brie has been through more than any of us can imagine. She needs sleep and time to recover. Let's save questions for later."

Although unsatisfied by Sir's suggestion, her father eventually nodded to him, then turned to Brie. "You know I love you, little girl."

She muttered quietly, "I know, Daddy."

"Mama!"

Brie's face lit up when she saw Hope toddling toward her with Shadow following behind. Leaning down, Brie held out her arms to her daughter.

Her heart burst with joy when she was able to sweep Hope up in her arms. Hope hugged her neck so tightly that Brie could barely breathe, but she didn't mind.

Holding Hope had some kind of magical power over Brie. The uneasiness that had been tormenting her since leaving the compound instantly lifted. "I've missed you, sweet pea!"

Hope giggled as Brie kissed her all over.

Turning to her father, Brie asked, "Where's Antony?"

"He's upstairs napping. Would you like me to get him?"

"I'll do it," Sir insisted.

Brie closed her eyes, twisting where she stood as she held Hope close—purposely losing herself in her daughter's love and innocent joy.

She was conscious of the fact that her father was standing beside her in uncomfortable silence. He was kind enough not to interrupt the precious moment between her and her child.

Squeezing Hope a little tighter, Brie finally opened her eyes and looked out the window to the shore. The waves were rolling in as they always had. She found it comforting that they remained unaffected by any outside influence—just like Sir's love.

She thought back to the poem he'd left on her pillow the day she had returned from the hospital after giving birth to Hope.

To the mother of my child.
I love you, Brianna.
You are my life.
My love.
My hope.
Be confident in my love for you.
It is eternal and constant
Like the waves of the ocean.
~Thane Davis

The waves would always remind Brie of the strength of his love, and she was grateful they had the power to soothe her battered soul now.

Everything will be okay, she told herself.

"Here you go, sweetheart," her mom announced sweetly, holding out a sandwich on a plate. "There's nothing like a PB&J to make everything better."

Brie chuckled. That had been her mother's signature remedy whenever she had been hurt as a kid—whether it was from falling off her bike, getting sick, or having her young heart broken by a boy.

She understood the message behind her mom fixing the simple dish and was touched. Moving Hope to her hip, Brie took the plate and smiled hesitantly. "Thanks, Mom."

"I'll make you as many as you need. A hundred if you want!"

"Heck, I can run to the store right now and clean them out," her father offered.

Brie giggled softly in response, wanting them to know she appreciated their desire to comfort her.

"He's changed and ready to see his mama," Sir announced, walking up to Brie.

"There's my baby boy…" Brie cooed.

Sir transferred the child to her and gave Hope a big hug. "It's good to have Mommy back home. Isn't it, my little angel?"

Tears came to Brie's eyes when she took in Antony's beautiful baby smell. "Oh, how I've missed you, sweet boy," she whispered.

Antony completely melted her heart when he smiled up at her. She held him against her chest and gazed lovingly at Sir. Brie knew in her soul that the love she had for her little family had the power to heal her heart—it was an indomitable force no evil could withstand.

Brie could see the concern etched into Sir's face and mouthed, *I'm going to be okay.*

He nodded, then turned and offered to get everyone a drink.

Still feeling uneasy, Brie smiled uncomfortably at her parents. Suddenly, she felt a furry body rub against her leg. The big black cat looked up at her, surprising her with the intensity of his gaze. It seemed like Shadow could sense something was wrong.

He sat down on his haunches and meowed at her.

"Are you hungry?" she asked him.

"We fed him this morning," her mother assured her.

Shadow's tail twitched back and forth and he meowed even louder.

Brie shrugged. "I don't know what you want, buddy."

The cat's tail swished faster as he continued to meow at her. Perplexed, Brie walked to the couch with Shadow following close behind. The moment Brie sat down, he jumped on the couch—which was something he was never allowed to do.

Before she could protest, the cat crawled into her lap and began purring loudly while he curled up beside Antony. She looked down at her son and the big black cat and absently began stroking the animal's soft fur.

Brie was profoundly comforted by the rhythmic rumble of his purr.

Sir stared at the cat with gratitude, choosing not to scold him. "This is one time when disobeying the rules is completely justified."

After her parents left, Brie asked Sir a question that had been troubling her ever since her rescue. "Why didn't Rytsar come? It's not like him at all."

Sir sighed heavily, obviously uncomfortable with her question. "Durov will tell you when the time is right."

Brie frowned, concerned by his strange response. "What is he keeping from me, Sir?"

Putting his hands on her shoulders, Sir looked deep into her eyes. "Now is not the time, Brie. Trust me."

She shook her head angrily. "I don't care. I need to know!"

To her utter frustration, Sir wouldn't budge. However, he did take his phone from his pocket and held it out to her. "I think you should talk to him yourself."

With a sigh of exasperation, Brie dialed the number and waited for Rytsar to pick up.

When he answered he immediately asked, "How is she, *moy droog*?"

Hearing Rytsar's low voice with that thick Russian accent warmed her head to toe. "It's me, Rytsar."

"*Radost moya!*" he cried out in surprise. "I cannot tell you how good it is to hear your voice."

Brie couldn't help smiling, despite the serious nature of her call. "I feel the same."

"I know better than to ask how you are doing when you've just been through hell. So, instead, tell me how are *moye solntse* and *moy gordost*?"

Brie glanced at Hope and Antony playing on the floor and grinned at them. "They are the most perfect beings in the world."

He chuckled. "*Da*, they are."

Brie let out a nervous sigh, building up the courage to ask. "Rytsar…why aren't you here?"

The Russian was silent for a moment, then he let out

an agonized groan. "It is torture not being with you right now."

"Then come," she begged.

He answered somberly, "I told you. I cannot."

"Why?" Brie demanded, unwilling to be left in the dark any longer.

"I promise I will reveal all when the time is right."

Brie growled. "Sir said the same thing, but it's not fair! I deserve to know the secret you are keeping from me."

"*Nyet.* It is my right to keep it from you until I deem it appropriate."

His refusal only frustrated her more. "I'll go crazy not knowing! You know I have a vivid imagination."

"I know you do…" he stated humorously. "I've read your fantasy journal."

She pursed her lips. "Don't try to distract me."

Rytsar paused for a moment before asking, "Would you agree that your Master knows you well?"

Brie sighed. "Of course."

"And I know you well."

"You do," she agreed reluctantly.

"Then I need you to trust us both."

Brie did not care for his answer and protested, "I think you should kneel on rice as punishment for keeping things from me."

"I would willingly do so, *radost moya*, but I would still refuse to tell you."

A wild thought flew through her mind and she blurted, "Rytsar…are you secretly engaged?"

He broke out in uproarious laughter. "Is that what

you think?"

"I don't know…" she stammered, equally embarrassed and grateful that it was not the case.

"I will not play twenty questions with you," he stated firmly. "You must know the only girl who has captured my heart is *moye solntse*."

Brie smiled grudgingly at his answer.

Rytsar's voice grew serious again. "When the time is right, I promise I will tell you. Until then, you must trust that your Master and I have only your best interests at heart."

"I'm so not satisfied by that explanation—at all," she complained.

"As a sadist, I admit that pleases me."

She rolled her eyes. "You are truly wicked, Anton Durov."

"But you still love me," he teased.

"I do. God help me."

The pitch of his voice rose in concern when he asked, "When you are ready, *radost moya*, I need you to tell me everything that happened with Holloway."

Chills ran down Brie's spine when she heard the man's name. "I will…" she agreed hesitantly, then added, "…when I see you in person."

Rytsar groaned again. "I make you a solemn vow to come as soon as I can."

"Tomorrow?" she asked half-jokingly.

"If God wills it," he replied, "but not until then."

Brie growled in exasperation. "I hope this secret is worth the torment it is causing me."

"I would have told you if it were not."

She was about to hang up, but decided to throw out one last guess, knowing it was guaranteed to evoke an instinctual response from him. "Is it Lilly?"

Rytsar chuckled. "I told you I wasn't playing twenty questions, *radost moya.*"

Brie sighed in defeat. Although she would not be getting any answers today, at least she had two fewer things to worry about—Lilly and losing Rytsar to a secret marriage.

She handed Sir back the phone. "I'm still miffed about being left in the dark, but Rytsar is right about one thing."

"What's that?"

"Even though you and I promised never to keep things from each other…" She met Sir's gaze and declared fervently, "I trust you."

After spending the day with the children and being pampered with a delicious meal Sir lovingly prepared for her that night, Brie found it difficult to stay awake.

"Let me put the children to bed before I tuck you in, babygirl," Sir told her.

Brie loved the sound of that and smiled. "That would be wonderful, Sir."

When he returned to her, Brie could barely keep her eyes open as he guided her to the bedroom. After she lay down, she sighed in contentment as she made a mock snow angel on the bed. "I never appreciated how sinfully comfortable beds are."

He silently undressed her before undressing himself and slipping into bed beside her. Spooning against her body, Sir put his arms around her and nuzzled her neck. "I'll take care of the children in the morning so you can sleep as long as you need."

She turned her head to kiss him on the lips. "My hero in every sense of the word."

He smiled, murmuring, "Go to sleep now."

Brie laid her head back on the pillow and closed her eyes. Being home, wrapped in Sir's arms, felt like a wonderful dream.

But, as she floated between consciousness and slumber, Brie heard his far-off call.

"Hey, little songbird…"

Dark Melody

Despite lying in a comfortable bed beside Sir, sleep proved nearly impossible for Brie. She was unable to stop those horrible lyrics from playing over and over again in her mind.

It made for a fitful sleep that provided her little rest. As soon as the sky lightened with predawn, Brie gave up on trying to sleep altogether and quietly slipped out of bed.

She headed up to the nursery and stood beside Antony's crib, watching him as he slept. The look on his sweet face was so peaceful and innocent that it helped combat the feelings of helplessness and terror, although it could not quiet the song in her head.

Brie let out a shriek when she felt a hand on her shoulder. Antony's eyes instantly popped open, and he started to wail.

"I'm sorry I startled you, babygirl," Sir apologized, picking up the baby to comfort him.

The lyrics grew even louder in Brie's head, making it

difficult for her to think. "You scared me."

"That's obvious," he whispered, patting Antony's back to get him to quiet down. "Were you able to get any sleep?"

"Some." Brie looked at her son sorrowfully. "I didn't mean to wake my little boy."

"No harm done," Sir assured her. He laid Antony back down in the crib and covered him with the blanket. Taking Brie's hand, he led her out of the room.

Once they were downstairs, he asked, "Would you like to go back to bed?"

"No," Brie replied, although she was desperate for rest. With the song still playing in her head, she knew sleep was impossible.

"Nonna's hot chocolate, then?"

She looked at him gratefully. "That would be perfect, Sir."

Brie watched as he made his grandmother's drink. His movements were fluid and concise as he grated the dark chocolate and sprinkled it into the double boiler. Her mouth started to water when he poured the melted chocolate into the pot of warm milk. Stirring it slowly, he glanced at her and smiled.

That tender smile melted her heart.

Pouring the hot chocolate into two mugs, Sir added a dash of cinnamon on top of both and walked to her, holding the mugs. "Let's watch the sunrise together," he suggested.

Handing the mugs to her, Sir grabbed a throw blanket from the couch. She followed him out back and watched as he pulled the outdoor loveseat over to get a better view of the ocean.

Brie sighed in contentment, snuggling up against him when he covered her in the blanket. She wrapped her hands around the hot mug and sighed happily. "This is nice."

Sir nodded as he stared out at the ocean.

Because it was so early, no one was on the beach. It made the moment intimate and cozy. "This reminds me of when we watched the sunrise in Russia," Brie murmured before taking a sip of the decadent chocolate.

"I agree. Although they are a world apart, watching the sun announce the start of a new day has a profound impact."

"It does, Sir."

They sat there in silence, listening to the waves as the predawn sky slowly changed in color as the sun rising in the east infused the clouds in the west with its brilliance.

It was peaceful and timeless.

Thankfully, the song had retreated to the background, giving her a moment of peace. However, something was still weighing on her mind.

"Have you spoken to Mary, Sir?"

"Not personally. Why?"

"I'm worried about her."

"Then you should talk to her yourself. I believe you both would benefit from seeing each other."

Brie shook her head. "I can't do that."

He looked at her, cocking his head questioningly. "Why not?"

Her heart began to race when she admitted her guilt over the role she'd played in Mary's violent punishment—and Mary's reaction to it. She understood why Mary hated her now.

Turning her head to stare at the ocean, Brie said sadly, "Mary couldn't even look at me after we were rescued."

Sir squeezed her tight. "I don't think that was the reason for her distance."

Brie frowned. "Although I didn't know it at the time, my disobedience led to the punishment she received. I'm directly responsible for every lash that cut her back."

"Holloway is responsible, not you. I'm certain Miss Wilson understands that," Sir stated firmly. "The fact you question it concerns me."

She looked down at her empty mug and had to hide her flinch when the song started up again.

"Hey, little songbird…"

After the sunrise, Sir insisted Brie return to bed for some much-needed rest. After taking a warm, soothing bath, Sir tucked her into bed and kissed her on the forehead.

"The only thing I need is for you to sleep."

She nodded and closed her eyes, fighting hard to block out the hated song. Just as she was about to drift off, she heard a hard knock on the front door.

Brie bolted upright when she heard her father shout, "Open up!"

Remaining in bed, she heard her mother tell Sir, "After seeing how thin Brie is, I cooked all of her favorite breakfast foods."

Brie slipped out of bed and grabbed her robe. Wrapping the tie around her waist, she cinched it up before walking out of the bedroom.

She was surprised to see an expansive spread of breakfast dishes on the counter in the kitchen. "What's all this?"

"I couldn't fall asleep last night, sweetheart," her mother explained. "I needed something to do, so I cooked you a nice breakfast. What started as a breakfast casserole soon became…" She gestured to all the food with a sheepish grin. "…this."

Brie shook her head and laughed. "There's no possible way I can eat all of this."

Her mother shrugged good-naturedly and turned to Sir. "Thane, I know you are just going to love this one," she said proudly, pointing to the casserole. "It's an all-American breakfast rolled into one delicious dish. It's full of eggs, hash browns, bacon, and cheese, and I added slices of tomatoes on top because I know how you like to eat healthy."

Sir stared at the casserole dish and pursed his lips. "Unfortunately, my stomach is feeling unsettled this morning."

"I'm so sorry to hear that," her mother exclaimed, looking at Sir with motherly concern. "Luckily, this casserole tastes even better the next morning. But I'd be happy to make you some oatmeal to settle your stomach, if you like."

During their conversation, Brie noticed her father staring at her intensely. So intently, in fact, it was starting to make her extremely uncomfortable.

"What's wrong, Daddy?"

Before he could answer, there was a loud commotion outside. Sir walked briskly to the front window and pulled back the curtain. "Fuck…"

Suddenly frightened, Brie whimpered, "What's happening, Sir?"

He turned to meet her gaze. "The press is here."

Brie hurried to the window and groaned when she saw several news vans parked down the street and a crowd of reporters setting up.

She looked at Sir, asking fearfully, "Why are they here?"

"I'll tell you why they are here," her father stated, picking up the newspaper he'd brought and shaking it in his hand. "Everyone wants to know what really happened to the people who were rescued, because what they are describing in this article is beyond horrific."

Brie's stomach twisted. Glancing again at the growing number of reporters gathering outside, she asked Sir, "Can't we demand that they leave?"

"Unfortunately, I am very familiar with the laws concerning the press, babygirl. They have the right to camp out on the public sidewalk in front of our house." He glanced down at her. "We can do nothing unless they trespass on our property."

Brie suddenly felt lightheaded and dizzy. "Sir…" she whispered.

He barely caught her before she hit the floor. Sweeping her into his arms, he carried Brie back to the bedroom. "You must rest. Stay in bed while I take care of this."

Brie was surprised to hear her parents leave the house with Sir. Curiosity got the best of her and she snuck to the window, slowly pulling back the curtain to take a peek.

Sir was being unusually dramatic, giving both her mother and father each a long hug before watching them drive off. Then he nodded to the reporters before heading back into the house.

Hurrying back to bed, Brie slipped under the covers and waited. She was surprised when she heard clinking sounds as Sir moved about in the kitchen. When he left the house again, Brie crept back to the window and watched as he walked straight up to the reporters and started handing out the dished-up food her mother had brought.

He returned to the house several times to make sure everyone received something to eat, then he put his arms behind his back and spoke to them with a serious look on his face. The moment he turned to point back at the house, Brie let go of the curtain and stood still, holding her breath.

To her surprise, she soon heard one of the vans drive off. Curious, Brie risked another peek. Brie's jaw dropped when she saw many of the reporters handing Sir something before gathering their equipment and walking away from the house.

She wondered what he could have possibly said to garner such a response.

Before Sir caught at the window, she slipped back into bed. It wasn't long before she heard Sir return and shut the front door. She held her breath when she heard his footsteps heading to their bedroom.

Knowing she'd been caught, Brie sat up in bed to await her fate.

Sir walked into the room, holding a plate of her mom's food. He smirked as he placed the plate on the nightstand beside her. "I saw you at the window."

She blushed. "I'm sorry, Sir. But you had those reporters eating out of your hand. How did you get them all to go away?"

"Not all of them, but the majority are gone," he replied. She looked at Sir in amazement as he explained, "I needed time to think, so I asked your parents to leave. Knowing the press would be watching our every move, I convinced your parents it was important we present a united front without speaking to them. To do that, we played out an emotional goodbye before they drove off.

"When I returned to the house and looked at all the food your mother had cooked, I was struck with an idea on how it could be put to good use. From my personal experience I know that fighting the press only causes problems, so I decided on a different approach. Since the reporters arrived here so early this morning, I assumed most of them hadn't had time to grab breakfast before heading out."

Sir walked to the window, pulling back the curtain to look at the few who remained. "After buttering them up with food, I appealed to them as a husband concerned about his wife's mental health. I explained that you were unable to make any statements at this time, but if they gave me their business cards and left immediately, I would call to invite each of them into the house when you were ready to speak."

Sir turned to her. "That means anyone who remains here will be left standing on the sidewalk should you ever decide to make a statement. Otherwise, they will be trespassing."

She stared at him in awe. "You're brilliant!"

He shrugged. "I'm glad the harassment I've suffered from the press could serve some purpose." Sir walked back to the bed and leaned down, kissing Brie gently on the lips.

"Naturally, all this ruckus woke up the children. So, fill up on your mother's food and try to get some sleep. Know this, babygirl. I will do everything in my power to protect your recovery."

Tears of gratitude filled her eyes as she watched Sir leave. Brie gingerly picked up the fork and took a small bite of her mom's casserole.

While she chewed it, Brie suddenly shivered when the far-off song start up again, its dark melody echoing in her mind.

Inner Power

After several weeks and numerous therapy sessions with Dr. Reinstrum, Brie found she was still struggling.

The only thing that brought her any joy was watching her kids play. She spent hours on the floor, observing but without the energy to join them. When she heard her phone ring, she glanced at it listlessly and saw it was Lea. She let it continue to ring, not interested in talking to anyone.

Not even Lea.

Nothing seemed to matter anymore—not her friends, her films, or even her future.

Brie felt disconnected from the world as if a switch had been turned off, and all that remained was the shell of the person she once was. She didn't recognize herself anymore.

Sir walked into the room to find her lying on the floor with her head propped up on a pillow, staring at the ceiling.

"Come, sit here with me," he told her, walking to the couch and patting the spot beside him.

Brie pushed herself off the floor and sat down next to him, asking, "What's this about, Sir?"

"I've noticed something that concerns me, and I care too much to ignore it any longer."

She swallowed nervously, waiting for him to continue.

Caressing her cheek lightly, he explained, "Holloway intended to steal a part of you and claim it for his own."

Brie nodded.

"In self-defense, you've distanced yourself from your submissive side, believing it is somehow tied to the perversity Holloway forced you to endure." Sir smiled at her gently. "But that is not your truth, babygirl."

With her bottom lip trembling, she whispered in desperation, "How do I get it back?"

Sir stood up and faced her. "When you are ready, Miss Bennett, you and I will scene together."

Brie smiled the moment she heard her maiden name. It hinted to the beginning of her journey into BDSM, when she started at the Training Center.

"Although I am responsible for the scene, you will approve each tool I plan to use beforehand. I will also ask your permission whenever I switch to a new instrument during the scene. *You* will be in complete control."

Brie nodded, warming up to the idea.

But Sir cautioned her. "I don't want you to agree to our session until you are confident you are ready. The last thing we want is to set you back in any way."

"Agreed, Sir." She paused for a moment before asking, "Do you think it will work?"

"It may take time to rebuild the level of trust we once had, but Baron assures me it will work."

She knew then that Sir had spoken to Baron, a Dominant who specialized in working with submissives who were victims of abuse. It renewed Brie's hope even more.

Without that essential part of herself, it made sense that she felt completely lost. "I'm grateful to you, Sir."

He looked down at her tenderly. "Why?"

"For anticipating my need and finding a way to fulfill it."

He chuckled. "That's my duty as your Dominant."

Brie stood up and wrapped her arms around him, pressing her head against his chest. "The depth of your understanding and love astounds me."

"I am a condor, and you are my chosen mate."

The power behind his words humbled Brie. He had chosen her over all the other women he'd met, and his loyalty to her was unquestioned.

"I wish Mary could accept this kind of love," she murmured. "It's heartbreaking to think she chose that monster over Faelan…"

"I understand you are worried about Miss Wilson and want to assure you that Captain and Candy are devoted to her well-being. I have every confidence she will eventually recover from the trauma she's suffered."

Brie looked at him sadly, her voice trembling when she said, "The violent punishment she endured on my behalf will forever haunt me, Sir."

"Brie," he stated firmly, "Miss Wilson did not suffer because of anything you did or didn't do. That responsibility lies squarely on Holloway's shoulders. It had nothing to do with you."

He cupped her chin and gazed into her eyes. "Surely you understand that."

Swimming in guilt, Brie confessed, "If Mary hadn't helped me with the documentary, none of this would have happened." She lowered her eyes. "And if I had truly listened to her when she warned me how ruthless Holloway was, maybe…I would have been more cautious after I humiliated him in front of his peers."

Tears fell down her cheeks when she told him, "Maybe I could have prevented Mary from becoming the primary focus in his revenge against me."

Sir put his arms around her. "Miss Wilson chose to help you. You never asked her to get involved. That was a choice she'd made for her own reasons."

"Mary can't even look at me now, Sir. And I can't blame her. Everything she suffered was because of Holloway's hatred for me."

"You know that's not true. Holloway groomed her since she was a child. Whether or not you were in the picture, Holloway already had his claws in her. Based on what we witnessed at the compound, his perversity went far beyond you—or his need for revenge."

She growled fiercely. "If I could, I would take it all back! I would never have filmed the original documentary and gotten involved with him."

"Babygirl," Sir stated calmly, "you are not listening to me. Whether you had filmed it or not, Mary's future would have still been tied to Holloway. The outcome may have played out differently, but Holloway's intentions toward her were never honorable." His voice became dark when he added, "The man has no soul."

Brie shuddered. "Mary and I experienced that firsthand…"

Sir enfolded her in his embrace and vowed, "If I ever come face to face with that man, regardless of where we meet, I will kill him with my bare hands."

Brie was unprepared when the doorbell rang later that afternoon. She peeked outside to find Marquis Gray standing on the porch.

The man was intimidating because of his uncanny ability to see straight into her soul. So, it was with some trepidation that she opened the door to welcome him in.

Feeling uncomfortably vulnerable in his presence, she immediately lowered her eyes to avoid his gaze and stammered, "I didn't realize you were coming to visit."

"I was actually headed to a meeting but felt a calling to come here instead." When she failed to reply, Marquis Gray stated warmly, "There is no reason to fear me, pearl."

Brie glanced up, surprised he had called her by the pet name he'd used when she was training at the Center. It instantly brought back memories of her first session with him and his flogger.

She had never forgotten that the talented Dom had been able to open her eyes to the depth of her inner power during that scene.

"May I come in?"

"Of course," she replied, embarrassed by her lack of decorum. Opening the door wider, she gestured for him to enter.

"I am surprised to see you here, Gray," Sir stated, walking out of his office.

The ghostly pale Dom nodded. "I felt a sudden urge to stop by."

Glancing at Brie, Sir asked her, "Are you comfortable having visitors, babygirl?"

Although it was unsettling to be near Marquis Gray, she deeply respected the man. He had always been kind and encouraging to her.

"Honestly, no," she answered. Raising her gaze, she looked directly into the trainer's eyes. "However, I will make an exception for Marquis Gray."

He surprised her by flashing a rare smile. "I am glad to hear it."

"Would you two like some privacy?" Sir asked them.

Marquis turned to Brie. "Actually, I was wondering if Mrs. Davis would like to take a walk on the beach."

She smiled shyly, happy for the suggestion. "That would be a welcomed distraction, Marquis Gray."

"Fine," Sir replied. "I'll return to my office then."

Hope peeked her head out and stared at Marquis with wide eyes.

The trainer chuckled. "I see you have an assistant working with you."

Sir glanced back at his daughter and smiled tenderly. "Both children have proved an invaluable addition to my staff."

Brie explained to Marquis, "Sir has been watching over the children while I…recover."

Marquis nodded. "I would expect no less from Sir Davis."

Wasting no time, Marquis Gray held out his arm to Brie. "Shall we?"

She nodded, glancing back at Sir nervously as they left.

Her handsome Master picked up Hope and held her hand, waving it at Brie. "Enjoy your walk, Mommy."

It was so adorable that Brie giggled.

She could never have imagined that the serious Dom who first collared her would make such a devoted family man. Brie instantly thought of Alonzo and realized she was catching a glimpse of the father Sir once knew and loved. It was a beautiful testament to the man that his fathering skills lived on in his son.

Marquis opened the door and guided Brie through it. "Why don't we take our shoes off so we can properly enjoy the sand?"

Brie smiled shyly, surprised by his suggestion. Quickly slipping off her sandals, she offered to help him with his dress shoes.

"Certainly, Mrs. Davis."

Brie knelt to untie the laces of his shoes. Setting them to the side, she removed his socks, stuffing them in the shoes.

"Thank you."

She smiled at him as she stood back up. "My pleasure, Marquis Gray."

"You may call me Asher."

Brie stared at him, trying to hide her shock. The trainer seldom allowed people to call him by his given name. "Thank you…Asher."

He nodded, holding out his arm to her again.

Together, they headed toward the waterline before starting down the beach. Marquis was silent for a long time, leaving Brie to wonder why he had come.

The other beachgoers couldn't help staring at Marquis as they passed. "It's not often you see a man dressed in a suit walking down the beach," Brie joked, finally breaking the silence.

Marquis nodded curtly to the female jogger gawking at him as she ran by. To Brie, he said, "Had I known where the day was headed, I would have chosen more casual clothing, I assure you."

Brie giggled. "Well, you certainly look distinguished, Marquis—" Instantly correcting herself, she amended, "I mean, Asher."

He looked down at his pale feet and said in a serious tone, "I ought to lay out more."

Brie strained to hold back the laughter as she envisioned the ghostly pale trainer tanning on the beach in a Speedo.

"It's okay to laugh, Mrs. Davis. I meant it as a joke."

She burst out in giggles. "I love your sense of humor. It's so understated that it hits you when you least expect it."

He patted her hand as they continued to walk down the beach. What started as uncomfortable silence soon became a tranquil communion as they followed the water line together.

Finally, he asked, "How are you doing—really?"

Brie shivered as the horrors she experienced instantly came flooding back. She took a moment to answer him. "I'm struggling, Asher."

"It's only natural after the trauma you've suffered, but I sense…"

She looked at him, suddenly feeling as if she couldn't breathe.

"…there's something more."

Tears pricked her eyes when she confessed, "I think I'm going crazy."

Marquis furrowed his brow. "How so?"

Brie's throat closed up, leaving her to struggle to force out the words. "I can't make it stop." The melody suddenly started up again, louder than before. She put her hands to her ears, trying to drown out the lyrics.

"I just want the song to stop!" she screamed.

"Look at me," Marquis commanded.

When she failed to obey him, he took her hands and lowered them to her sides. "Look at me, pearl."

Brie opened her eyes, unable to hide her agony.

Marquis didn't flinch when Brie met his powerful gaze.

She started trembling uncontrollably, the intensity of his gaze almost too painful to bear.

With time, however, she noticed the lyrics becoming more distant. Marquis did not release her from his gaze until the hateful song had completely faded away.

Brie blinked several times and then cried in relief, "It's gone!"

Marquis nodded, urging her to continue walking with

him. They headed down the beach as if nothing had happened. Soon, the tranquility she'd felt before returned.

"How did you do that, Asher?"

"I did nothing. I simply helped you focus until you were able to drown it out yourself."

She shook her head. "But I've been trying to do that ever since I came back. I even told my therapist about it and he wasn't able to help."

"You are much stronger than you give yourself credit for," Marquis insisted.

She felt the prickling sensation she associated with important moments in her life and repeated his words to herself.

You are much stronger than you give yourself credit for.

"I knew it the moment we met," Marquis Gray continued.

Brie frowned. "I don't feel strong, Asher—far from it."

"You were in a battle for your life, pearl. It's only natural that a warrior needs time to heal from her battle wounds." He touched her forehead. "Including those wounds that cannot be seen."

Her chin trembled when she admitted, "I'm surrounded by the people I love the most, and yet…I feel lost. I don't think I will ever be normal again."

Marquis Gray stopped and grazed her cheek with the back of his hand. "You are not the person you were before. You must come to terms with that. However, you can move forward as a new creation, stronger than you were. Just as bodybuilders damage their muscle fibers to build stronger muscles, you can take the tragic things you've experienced to build a stronger version of yourself."

Brie felt that prickling sensation again. "I believe you, Asher."

He smiled, patting her lightly on the back as he turned her around and headed back to the house. "It will take time, pearl. Be patient with yourself."

Reclaiming Her

Although her situation hadn't changed, Brie felt empowered after speaking with Marquis. She continued to think about their conversation for weeks after. It wasn't lost on her that Marquis had called her 'pearl', the name he used while training her, and Brie took it as a sign.

After putting Antony down for a nap, she walked into Sir's office to find Hope on the floor, clipping bows to Shadow's black fur. The huge animal looked comical covered in pink and purple bows, but he endured Hope's attention like a champ.

Knocking on the door frame, Brie announced, "I've made a decision, Sir."

He turned from his desk to face her. "About what?"

She suddenly felt butterflies as she stared into those magnetic eyes. "I want to scene with you."

Sir raised an eyebrow. "You are sure?"

"I haven't been more certain about anything in my life."

"Excellent, Miss Bennett. We will discuss the tools I'll be using."

Brie shivered. For some reason, she suddenly felt bashful, as if this was to be her first time scening with him. It came as a shock to her since she was not only his submissive but also the mother of his two children.

"Just to be clear, we will not be scening tonight," Sir stated. "I need adequate time to plan our session."

Brie nodded, overcome with nervous anticipation. She suddenly felt…alive again.

"I understand, Sir." As she turned to leave, she looked back and smiled shyly. "Thank you."

Her heart melted when he winked at her.

Brie walked away, marveling at the fact that Sir's patience and foresight had been able to rekindle those feelings inside of her.

Maybe, just maybe, she could reclaim the very thing Holloway had tried so violently to destroy.

Friday night, Sir joined Brie and the kids in the dining room. He was dressed in his expensive Italian suit. He looked so fine that she struggled to keep her wits about her.

"Daddy pretty!" Hope cried enthusiastically, clapping her hands.

"Why thank you, little angel," Sir replied, bending down to kiss her on the cheek.

Brie stared at him, murmuring, "I have to agree with

Hope…"

Sir sat down beside Brie and gave her a long, lingering look before dishing up his daughter's plate.

Brie couldn't take her eyes off Sir, certain that tonight would be the night.

"You look a little flushed, my dear. Are you feeling well?" he asked with a smirk.

Brie waved her hand back and forth, fanning herself. "It suddenly got hot in here."

"You don't say?" He smiled charmingly. "Would you like some pasta, Miss Bennett?"

Hearing him call her by her maiden name made the butterflies start up again because it removed any doubt about what Sir planned for tonight.

"I would love that. Thank you," she answered breathlessly.

As Sir handed her the bowl of pasta, his hand grazed hers. It was like a bolt of electricity passing between them, and Brie nearly dropped the dish.

"Are you sure you're okay?"

She just nodded, blushing profusely.

While the two of them were clearing the table after dinner, Sir leaned in close. "I have planned something special for you after the children go to bed."

Even though she knew every tool that he would be using tonight, she was still buzzing with excitement.

Two hours later, after laying Antony down in his crib, Brie walked into Hope's room to find Sir on the floor with his jacket unbuttoned, reading aloud to her. Brie loved the sound of his deep voice as he read the familiar fairy tale about the little mermaid.

When he finished, Brie came in and tucked Hope in bed, and they both kissed her goodnight. Brie blew her a final kiss before she shut the door.

Sir leaned in to kiss Brie but stopped just centimeters from her mouth. In a dangerously seductive voice, he commanded, "Join me in the bedroom in five minutes, Miss Bennett."

Tingles coursed down her spine.

While she waited those few minutes in the hallway, Brie felt not only her anticipation growing but also her fear.

What if this failed tonight despite their best efforts? Could the psychological scars that Holloway inflicted cut so deeply that she would never know the joy of submission again?

That thought petrified her.

Brie stared at the entrance to their bedroom and chose to face her fear.

Standing straight with her shoulders pushed back and her head up, but still at a respectful angle, she walked into the bedroom.

She found the door to their secret room open with Sir standing beside it, holding out a red rose to her. "For my goddess."

Brie smiled graciously as she took the stunning rose from him, suddenly shy and nervous again.

Sensing her uneasiness, Sir reminded her, "You are in complete control, Miss Bennett. I encourage you to call out your safeword if needed."

Seeing the love reflected in his eyes renewed her courage. "I'm certain it won't come to that, Sir."

"Tonight, you will call me Master."

She felt a thrill repeating his title. "Master…"

Sir lifted her chin and placed a gentle kiss on her lips. "Now, that didn't hurt. Did it?"

"Not at all, Master," she answered, feeling giddy with love for him.

Escorting her into the playroom, he gestured to the table of tools he'd set out. Pointing to the rose in her hand, he told her, "We'll begin with the rose to stimulate your skin and then move on to the tools we both agreed to."

Brie looked down at the table.

Sir had carefully laid out the items: a set of jeweled nipple clamps, a sensual massage candle, a blindfold, and a beautiful glass butt plug with an artful pink rose painted inside the glass.

"Hold the rose while I undress you," he instructed.

Sir's undressing of her was like a sensual dance. He led her with his caresses as he slowly guided her clothes to the floor. Once she was naked, he stood back and looked at her with adoration.

When she looked into his eyes, she could see with clarity the vision he had of her—it was breathtaking and deeply humbling. "You honor me, Master."

His gaze grew softer. "I love everything about you—your passion, your mind, your body, your need…all of it."

Brie teared up, remembering the first time he'd confessed those words to her in the cold Russian snow. Sir lightly brushed her tears away, chiding, "No crying tonight."

Brie smiled demurely. "Yes, Master."

Sir took the rose from her and asked, "Color, Miss Bennett?"

Glancing at the beautiful rose, she giggled. "Definitely green, Master."

Sir used the flower like an extension of his hand, grazing it lightly over her skin as he planted tender kisses on her shoulders and neck. After he brushed the soft petals against her breasts, he followed it up with a passionate kiss that left her utterly breathless.

He had her completely under his spell when he swept Brie off her feet and placed her on the bondage table.

Per their agreement, no bindings were being used during the scene. Although she enjoyed the feeling of helplessness that bondage inspired, Sir was concerned it might trigger her after the trauma she'd endured.

Holding up the massage candle, he asked her, "Color, Miss Bennett?"

She smiled as she stared at the black jar with a spout, the wick barely peeking out above the rim. "A definite green, Master."

Sir lit a match and Brie watched as the wick burst into flame. Setting the candle back on the table, he stared at her as he unbuttoned his jacket and casually hung it on the St. Andrew's cross. Next, he loosened his silk tie and slipped it off, then slowly unbuttoned his shirt, exposing the hair on his manly chest. Undoing the buttons on his cuffs, Sir rolled up his sleeves, never breaking his gaze.

Brie always found it sexy to watch him prepare for a scene.

"I want to get comfortable for this," Sir stated, slipping off his dress shoes before unbuckling his belt and sliding it through his belt loops. He let it fall to the floor with a satisfying clank.

Walking up to the table, still dressed in his opened shirt and dress pants, Sir picked up the candle. Brie held her breath as she watched him slowly lift it to his lips and blow it out, leaving a wisp of smoke curling up from the wick.

"We begin with the massage."

Her heart raced a little as he tipped the jar slightly and the oil poured out. Even though she knew it was coming, she jumped when the warm oil first contacted her skin.

"Too hot?" he murmured huskily.

"Just right, Master," she assured him.

Sir poured the oil between her breasts and slowly trailed it down to her mound. He then set the candle back on the table. With his skilled hands, he began sensually spreading the warm oil over her skin. Although it was exceedingly pleasant, the magic didn't happen until he began massaging her body.

This wasn't a normal, relaxing massage. Sir's hands glided over her skin like liquid electricity, causing a tingling sensation wherever he touched her. What enchanted Brie even more was the reverent look in his eyes as he touched her. Sir wasn't just massaging her, he was making love to her body with his hands as he caressed her breasts and then moved lower to tease her mercilessly with those magical fingers.

Brie would never forget the way he massaged her that night. It was as if he was in the presence of the woman he had worshipped from afar, and he was now basking in the decadent pleasure of touching her for the first time.

It was exhilarating and had her dripping in excitement.

When he told her to turn onto her stomach, Brie thought she might just combust. While she did as he asked, Sir lit the candle again and waited patiently for it to heat up.

"I've always been mesmerized by that ass," he growled seductively, spanking it sensually several times. Each contact sent shivers of pleasure through her.

When he picked up the candle again and drizzled it over her buttocks, Brie moaned softly, certain she would burst into flames when he touched her again.

Sir meticulously covered her in the oil, then began to massage her shoulders, slowly making his way down to her ass. She moaned in pleasure when he began to squeeze and knead her buttocks, teasing her with his erotic touch.

Brie longed for him to take her anally, but his fingers only pressed against her tight rosette, never penetrating her.

His focused attention only made her ache for him more.

Once he had her whole body burning with need, Sir picked up the glass toy. "Color, Miss Bennett?"

"Fiery hot green," she moaned. His light chuckle only fanned the flames of her desire.

Sir poured more of the warm oil between the valley of her ass cheeks and then teased her with the glass toy until she begged, "Please, Master…"

"As you wish," he answered huskily, spreading her ass as he slowly pressed the warm glass into her.

Her pussy gushed with wetness as her body eagerly accepted the invasion of the butt plug. "Yes…"

"Damn, Miss Bennett," Sir stated in admiration, "That decorative addition suits you." He spanked her ass again, obviously turned on by the look of it.

Grabbing a wet cloth to clean his hands, Sir picked up the nipple clamps next. "Color?"

"Multiple shades of green, Master."

Sir held out his hand to her. "I want you standing for this one."

Brie grabbed the hand he offered and climbed off the table to face him.

"Hands above your head," he commanded huskily.

Brie clasped her wrists above her head and watched as Sir took one end of the jeweled tweezer-tip clamps and placed it around her left nipple. He tightened it enough to emulate the pressure of a man sucking hard on her nipple—not hard enough to cause pain, but just enough to make her pussy even wetter.

He placed the other clamp on her right nipple and adjusted it before pulling lightly on the jeweled chain attached to them. Brie moaned passionately, turned on by the dual stimulation of the wickedly sexy nipple clamps and glass butt plug.

Sir twirled her around several times in appreciation before he turned her to face the bondage table. Holding up the last item, he asked, "Color, Miss Bennett?"

Brie looked at the blindfold and said breathlessly,

"Green, green, green, Master."

She smiled as he placed the blindfold over her eyes and secured it. But, the moment he took his hands away, she froze as she was instantly catapulted back to that dark cell.

Sir instantly noticed the difference in her and removed the blindfold even before she said a word. He wrapped her in his arms, murmuring soothingly. "It's okay, babygirl. You did well tonight…"

Brie looked up at him, feeling defeated. "But I don't want it to end…"

Sir surprised Brie when he tossed the blindfold far away. "It doesn't have to end. You are in control, remember?"

Relief flooded through her. Brie was far too in love and aroused to deny her raging need for him. "Command me, Master," she begged.

Without missing a beat, he ordered, "Turn and face the table."

Brie immediately obeyed, trembling in anticipation as she waited for his next order.

"Lean against the table and spread your legs, Miss Bennett. Your Master is going to fuck you with that toy deep inside you while those pretty little nipple clamps sway in time with my thrusts."

"Yes," she purred enthusiastically, wiggling her ass to entice him.

"Naughty girl…" Sir growled, slapping her on the ass before he pressed his cock against her wet pussy and pushed it into her.

Brie used the table as leverage as she took his cock

deeper with every stroke. She felt a sense of triumph when her pussy started to pulse, warning her of an impending orgasm.

"I'm close…!" she cried out.

"I want you to come all over your Master's cock," Sir commanded.

Brie blissfully obeyed, fully embracing her climax while she listened to Sir roar in ecstasy as he reclaimed his beloved submissive.

Confrontation

Brie slept like a baby the entire night. The lyrics that had tortured her ever since her rescue had vanished and the scene last night had reignited her passion.

If that was true for her, then maybe Mary could find a way out of the darkness, too.

Sir smiled when she emerged from the bedroom. "Well, you look rested."

Brie saw he was rocking Antony in his arms and walked over to them. "Best sleep I've had since I don't know when."

"Glad to hear it."

"You are a miracle worker, Sir. Last night was pure magic!"

"I can't claim all the credit. My inspiration came from a certain muse with a shapely ass and delectable lips."

Brie glanced down at his crotch momentarily before meeting his gaze. "These lips long to show you their gratitude."

He adjusted his pants, growling under his breath. "Says my wife five minutes before my ten o'clock conference call."

Taking Antony from him, she laughed apologetically. "I'm sorry, Sir."

He leaned down to give her a quick kiss. "I forgive you, but I'm taking you up on that 'gratitude' later."

As she watched Sir retreat to his office, she called out, "I'm thinking of visiting Mary today."

He turned to face her. "I think that is an excellent plan, babygirl."

Brie nodded but sighed nervously after he shut his office door. "I just hope she'll talk to me…" she muttered under her breath.

Antony responded by holding up his hand. Brie nibbled lightly on his tiny fingers, making him smile. His toothless grin seemed to melt away all her worries.

That was the enchanting thing about children—they lived in the moment. The past and the future didn't matter, only what was happening in front of them now. "Maybe I should bring you with me so you can cheer up my friend, too," she declared, kissing his soft baby head.

Brie headed out to visit Mary shortly after lunch. She was feeling overly anxious because this was the first time she'd left the house on her own since the kidnapping. But, it was important to her. The idea of living her life in constant fear because of Holloway was not an option.

Out of the corner of her eye, she spied the last remaining reporter taking pictures of her as she backed the car out of the driveway. It distracted her enough that she almost knocked out their mailbox.

Brie stopped the car and closed her eyes, taking a deep breath. "You got this, Brianna." Opening her eyes again, she pulled forward and adjusted the car before pulling out again. Not giving the reporter another glance, Brie successfully backed out and onto the street, then headed on her way.

She was on a mission to see Mary, and *nothing* was going to stop her. But, as she pulled up to Captain's house, she noticed several reporters just outside their door. "Maybe this was a bad idea," she mumbled to herself when they started frantically taking pictures of her.

Her confidence started to crumble.

After all, why would Mary want to see her after the hell she had gone through? Hadn't she suffered enough on Brie's behalf?

Antony's happy little squeak from the backseat helped Brie make her decision. If there was any chance of salvaging their friendship, she had to take it.

Before she could change her mind, Brie got out and opened the car door to unbuckle her son, cooing sweetly. "How could Mary ever turn away your cute little face?"

She covered him with a blanket to stop the reporters from getting photos of her son. Then, ignoring their shouts and attempts to get her attention, Brie walked up to the house and rang the doorbell. She stood there fidgeting uncomfortably while she waited for Candy to answer the door.

After several moments, she laughed uncomfortably and whispered to her son, "I guess I should have called first to make sure they were home…"

Brie was surprised when Captain answered the door. He looked uncharacteristically shocked to see her and said in a severe whisper, "You were the last person I expected to see, Mrs. Davis."

She swallowed hard, realizing how foolish she'd been to think Mary would simply forgive her. "I'm sorry to disturb you, Captain. I'll just go…"

As she turned to leave, he said firmly, "Absolutely not."

Brie looked back at him in confusion.

Candy rushed to the door, crying happily, "Oh, my goodness, Brie. What a surprise to see you. And you brought the baby, too!"

Before Captain invited her in, he asked, "I assume you came to see Mary?"

"It's the whole reason I came." She lowered her eyes, stammering, "But…if she doesn't want to see me…" She sighed uncomfortably. "…I understand."

Captain let out an amused snort and glanced at Candy. Opening the door wider, he commanded, "Come in, Mrs. Davis."

Brie silently questioned the private exchange between the two, but she took solace in knowing that Captain would not have invited her in to their house if he didn't think she should be there.

They remained silent as Captain led Brie to the living room, but Candy glanced back at Brie with a welcoming smile.

"Take a seat," he ordered.

Brie immediately sat down on the couch.

"Wait here while I speak with leif."

Before leaving the room, he turned to Candy. "They'll require refreshments." He paused for a moment before adding, "And tissues, as well."

"Yes, Captain," Candy replied.

Candy gave Brie a big hug before heading into the kitchen, telling her, "This is such a wonderful surprise." She looked at Antony and murmured, "I can't believe how much he looks like his daddy!"

"I know," Brie agreed, grinning down at her son.

Her anxiety began to increase with each passing minute she sat there alone with her son after Candy left the room.

Brie listened carefully. Mary wasn't spewing profanities like the last time she'd visited. However, the house seemed eerily silent, and that did not bode well.

Antony stared up at her with wide eyes. His presence kept Brie rooted where she was, when all she wanted to do was run out the door.

The moment Brie heard Captain's boots announcing his return, a feeling of dread washed over her. He entered the room first and pointed to the chair beside Brie. "Leif, you will sit there and listen to what Mrs. Davis has come to say."

Mary looked at Captain pensively but did as he asked without making eye contact with Brie. Candy joined them a few moments later, placing a tray with two glasses of water and a plate of cookies on the coffee table. "I'm all out of iced tea, but I'd be happy to make you some coffee if you'd like."

Brie picked up one of the glasses and told her, "Water's perfect. Thank you."

Mary didn't say anything. She only gazed pleadingly at Captain.

"We'll leave you two alone now," he announced, holding out his arm to Candy to escort her out. Together, they left Brie alone with an obviously unhappy Mary.

Letting out a nervous sigh, Brie took a small sip of water before setting the glass back down. Mary still refused to look in Brie's direction, keeping her gaze focused on the wall in front of her.

It gave Brie the chance to stare openly at Mary.

Although she had dark circles under her eyes and her hair looked stringy and unwashed, Mary still looked striking, as if nothing could touch her beauty—not even the horrors of Greg Holloway.

It gave her hope for Mary. Just as she was about to reach out to touch her friend, Mary snapped, "Get it over with, bitch, so I can leave."

Brie expected the anger in Mary's voice, but it still cut her like a knife. She was mute for a moment. It suddenly occurred to her that this might be the last time she would ever be in the same room as Mary.

"M—" she started, but the huge lump in her throat strangled her voice. Brie knew their friendship was on the line and the next few minutes could define the rest of their future relationship. Taking a moment to recover, Brie tried again. "Mary...I'm sorry."

Mary frowned, turning her head to gape at Brie. "What. The. Fuck."

Brie swallowed back her tears, adding, "I understand why you never want to see me again."

Mary shook her head in disbelief. "Are you seriously

trying to fuck with me right now?"

Brie stared at her in bewilderment. "I—"

"Don't play me, bitch. I'm the reason you almost died. If I could turn back time, I never would have joined the Training Center. That way I could protect you from Greg."

Brie shook her head, certain she had misheard. "Mary, I thought you couldn't forgive me."

"Bitch, I thought the same."

The two stared at each other for several seconds and then burst out laughing in response to the absurd situation.

"You thought I came here to yell at you?" Brie laughed, tears running down her face.

Mary nodded. "Why else would you be here?"

"I was terrified of losing you."

She snorted. "That would be the best thing for you, idiot."

"Never," Brie declared, grabbing a tissue and handing it to her before getting one for herself. While she was dabbing her eyes, the reality of what they had been through suddenly hit Brie full force.

What started out as tears of laughter quickly disintegrated into ones of pain. "Oh, Mary…"

Mary got up and sat beside her on the couch. "I know…" She hugged Brie, trying not to disturb Antony. Sitting together in that awkward position, the horror they'd faced suddenly bubbled up to the surface. It spilled out in a torrent of tears as the two shared that unspeakable pain.

Mary reached over and grabbed the tissue box,

clutching it in her hand as the two of them continuously wiped the tears that refused to stop. It was a shared experience that only those who'd lived through the pain and suffering could understand.

"You're stronger than I thought, Stinks," Mary said, blowing her nose loudly.

"Me? I can't believe you are still standing. I saw what Venom did to you…" A burst of fresh tears started as Brie recalled how brutally Mary had been punished.

Mary calmly cleaned up her face before stating, "I discovered an untouched place inside of me back when I was a kid. No matter how bad the beatings got, my step-father could never hurt that part of me. *No one* can…"

Brie looked at her in admiration.

"No one, until you." Mary snarled. "Not being able to protect you was the most helpless I've ever felt. It was calculated on Greg's part—and far crueler than a fucking lashing."

Brie shuddered as she thought back on it. "Watching you take the punishment that was meant for me is something I can't forget."

Mary looked at her with red-rimmed eyes. "I planned to die that last night, you know. I would have done anything he asked to protect you."

Brie felt chills.

Mary looked down at Antony. "I wanted to make sure your kids didn't grow up without their mommy. No child deserves that."

Brie looked at Mary with compassion. "I wasn't about to watch you die. I vowed to see it until the bitter end so we could both get out alive."

Mary snorted. "Greg hated that about us. He couldn't stand the bond we shared because it threatened him." She growled. "That's why he used it as leverage against us. It had to be destroyed because it was something completely foreign to him."

Brie shouted angrily, "I hope to God he goes to the deepest, darkest part of hell, along with everyone involved!"

"They will," Mary stated with confidence. "And I plan to meet them there one day so I can fan the flames under their feet for all of eternity."

Brie realized Mary's intense hatred for Holloway had given her the strength to survive the horrific abuse. But it also tied her to him in a way that was unnatural and harmful to her soul.

Mary had literally fought demons trying to protect Brie.

"You are a good person."

Mary glared at her. "Shut the fuck up, Stinks."

Brie said nothing. She knew it might take years, maybe even decades, to unravel the damage Holloway had done to her friend. But Brie silently vowed to remain by Mary's side every step of the way.

Despite Holloway's hellish efforts and their own doubts about each other, their bond remained unbroken.

Cowboy Charm

Brie called Sir to let him know she was ready to head home. She didn't want him to worry about her.

While Captain was escorting Brie to her car, Brie was shocked to see twice as many reporters as before.

They started talking over each other, trying to get her to answer their questions.

"Is Miss Wilson on the verge of suicide?"

"Mrs. Davis, were you sexually assaulted by your kidnappers?"

"Is it true that this is all a PR stunt to garner attention for your latest documentary?"

Captain raised his hand and growled in a commanding voice that left no room for dissent, "There will be no further questions!"

Blessed silence reigned as Brie finished buckling Antony in his car seat. She then jumped into her car and thanked Captain.

He nodded to her, then glanced back at the reporters, daring any one of them to speak.

Brie had been excited to tell Sir about her visit with Mary, but the encounter with the reporters upset her. She found their questions unsettling.

When she arrived home, she was pleasantly surprised to see that the last remaining holdout had given up. Obviously, the reporter had a better story to pursue, and her street was now free of the press. It made coming home feel much more like the welcomed escape she'd always known.

When she opened the front door, she found Sir in the living room on all fours with Hope riding piggyback. "How did it go with Miss Wilson?" he asked amid Hope's delighted giggles.

"You were right, Sir. Mary needed me as much as I needed her."

He nodded, helping Hope down before getting up off the floor. "How is she faring?"

Brie knew that as her former trainer, Sir would never stop caring about Mary's well-being. "She blames herself for what happened."

"It seems to be a trait you both share."

She snorted sadly. "We laughed when we figured that out. It was funny until it wasn't..." She let out a ragged sigh. "No one really knows how much Mary has suffered. It goes way beyond anything I could imagine."

Sir walked over to Brie and wrapped an arm around her "Now that Holloway is behind bars, Miss Wilson can finally begin healing. It will take time, so you must have infinite patience with her."

Brie kissed his cheek. "Luckily, I have the best teacher."

"On that note, I have something I want to discuss with you. Last night was a positive step for us, but it's obvious we still have a way to go to build back the level of trust we once had."

"I agree, Sir," she answered forlornly.

"To that end, I have a proposal for you. I'd like to start with the basics and slowly build on them."

Her eyes lit up. "Like I experienced at the Submissive Training Center?"

"Exactly." Putting both arms around her, he asked, "How would you feel if I invited some of the Doms you have worked with in the past to play out rudimentary scenes structured to build your trust? They would take place here, in your territory, so to speak. And, just like last night, you would be in control. If at any moment you reached a point where you felt uncomfortable, you would simply call out your safeword and end the session."

She looked at him questioningly. "Why couldn't I do that with you, Sir?"

"I want to be your safety net, babygirl. I do not want to inadvertently become a trigger point for you."

Brie nodded, remembering the paralyzing fear she'd felt last night when he'd put the blindfold on.

"By using the same Dominants to play out past lessons, it's my hope your prior experience with them will help you overcome any potential triggers." He caressed her cheek. "I intend to move slowly with these lessons so that you only experience positive encounters as you build up trust."

She gazed into his eyes. "In every way, you support

me."

"I love you, téa. It's my honored duty to see that you thrive."

Not a man to procrastinate, Sir spoke to Brad Anderson and his girlfriend Shey on the phone. When Brie heard who Sir had picked to play out her first encounter, she immediately envisioned a bullwhip and knew it was way too soon to face such a challenge.

It was foolish of her to worry.

Not only did Sir know her well, but he had been the Headmaster of the entire Submissive Training Center. He understood the steps that needed to be taken to ensure her well-being, both physically and mentally.

Still, Brie was concerned that Shey would be upset by Sir's request. The girl had no idea that Master Anderson planned to propose to her because he had postponed his plans after Brie's kidnapping.

Poor Shey still had no idea she was dating a millionaire!

It gutted Brie knowing that Master Anderson had been forced to put their lives on hold.

"Anderson says he's happy to do it," Sir informed her after ending the call.

"And Shey's okay with it?"

He looked at her tenderly. "I don't think you realize how much your friends care about you, babygirl. Shey not only agreed but asked if there was anything else you needed."

It humbled Brie that all of her friends had respected her need for isolation, but had remained patiently waiting on the sidelines for a chance to help her.

"I should call Lea," she suddenly decided.

"Ms. Taylor would appreciate that. She has called me at least twice a day for updates on you."

"Why didn't you tell me, Sir?" Brie cried.

"I didn't want you to be motivated to call out of obligation, but from a genuine need to connect. Ms. Taylor agrees with me. She understands you need time to recover."

"My poor sweet friend!"

Brie immediately picked up her phone and dialed Lea's number.

"Oh, my gosh," Lea squeaked. "You called because you need to hear one of my jokes! I can't tell you how long I've been waiting for this moment, Stinky Cheese."

Brie loved that the first words out of Lea's mouth weren't questions about what had happened. Instead, she was drawing Brie back in with her humor. "I couldn't stand another minute without a laugh. Hit me, Lea."

"Did you hear about the county jail that separated the inmates based on if they were Dominants or submissives?"

"Can't say that I have," Brie answered gleefully, having no clue where the joke was headed.

"They had the place sorted top to bottom."

"Cute!" Needing more of the light banter, Brie insisted, "Hit me again."

Lea squealed in delight. "What do you call a color

that hasn't been invented yet?"

"Hmm…that's a good one. Give me a moment." Brie was stumped and blurted the first thing that came to mind. "Invisible?"

"Valiant effort, Stinky Cheese. But the correct answer is…" Lea drew it out, a total professional when it came to comedic timing. "A *pigment* of your imagination!"

Brie burst out in laughter. "That one was—"

Lea teased, "Go ahead. Tell me how lame my jokes are."

"Actually, I was going to say it was perfect."

"Aww…!" Lea cried happily. "You've never said that before."

Brie grinned. "It was really funny, Lea."

"I know. Heck, girl, I crack myself up at least two hundred times a day!"

Brie couldn't stop laughing and caught Sir staring at her. He winked, stating quietly, "It's good to hear you laugh again, babygirl," before walking out of the room.

Rather than describing the hell she'd endured, Brie spent the next hour asking Lea to catch her up on all the happenings in the community. From Lea's fabulous dates with Hunter and a new club opening up downtown, to Faelan being sighted at the beach at sunset with his little girl.

"Have you heard how he is doing?" Brie asked her.

"He seemed to be doing well and was ready to move out of Marquis Gray's house with his baby daughter. But that plan got put on hold after you and Mary disappeared."

Brie frowned. "I never considered how that would affect Faelan. Marquis didn't even mention his name when he visited."

"Because it's nothing you need to worry about, silly goose. You just need to take care of you right now."

"Did you hear that I visited Mary yesterday?"

Lea snorted. "Yeah, Brie. The whole world knows."

Brie suddenly felt the hairs rise on her neck. "What are you talking about?"

"Let's keep this call light," Lea begged.

"Please explain, Lea," she insisted.

Lea took a deep breath. "When the press reported that you went to see Mary, the media went into a feeding frenzy of speculation. I heard that one of the girls rescued even promised them an exclusive story."

"I knew it would happen eventually," Brie sighed. "I just hope she doesn't say too much. None of us should be forced to relive that nightmare just to entertain the public."

"I agree with you a hundred percent, girlfriend. That's why I'm not going to ask you a damn thing about it. You can share whatever you want when you want, or nothing at all! The only thing I care about—and let me repeat this so you don't miss it—the *only* thing I care about is you."

Brie felt the warmth of Lea's love and sighed contently. "I love you."

"I love you, too, Stinky Cheese. To the moon and back!"

"I know you care about Mary, too," Brie told her. "And I want you to hear it from me, not some reporter trying to make a headline. Captain and Candy are giving her the support she needs right now. Although she's really struggling, Mary is a survivor."

"That girl is like a cockroach, and I mean that in the best possible way."

Brie's chuckle was tinged with sadness. "Yeah, I can see that. No matter what she's suffered, Mary is too strong and fucking stubborn to ever give up."

"I appreciate you telling me. I was worried about Mary, but I knew she would never pick up the phone to call me for a joke."

Brie laughed, knowing it was true.

"Still, she really needs my jokes. Maybe I could just mail them to her?"

"I think that is a wonderful idea, my friend," Brie said.

Even if Mary never read any of the jokes, just knowing Lea was reaching out could make a difference.

Brie took a long, warm bath to relax and ready herself for her scene with Master Anderson. She was looking forward to the encounter and was excited by the simple scene he had planned.

Sir had already made arrangements with her parents for childcare and insisted on staying in his office with the door closed during their session. "I want you to know that I am here if you need me, but I do not want to act as a distraction."

"You could never be a distraction, Sir."

He smirked, slowly running his hand down the swell of her breast to her pelvis before grabbing her waist possessively.

Tingles coursed through her body. "I stand corrected."

He winked at her before glancing at his watch. "Anderson should be here in a few minutes. Take this time to ready yourself mentally for the scene ahead."

"I will, Sir."

After she watched his office door close, Brie went to kneel in the foyer to await his arrival. She closed her eyes, remembering the first time she'd met Master Anderson at the Training Center. He had been invited to serve on the panel in a temporary position because he planned on starting up a new training center in Colorado.

At the time nobody could have guessed that Master Anderson would soon take Sir's place on the panel after Thane stepped down as Headmaster to collar Brie at the end of her training.

Brie stilled those thoughts, concentrating instead on the scene about to take place. Although Master Anderson was incredibly funny and known for his practical jokes, when it came to playing out a BDSM scene together, he was a demanding Master.

It made submitting to him exhilarating and a little scary. She didn't want to disappoint him—or herself. To prepare, Brie not only knelt by the front door but also chose a pose that signified her willingness to submit.

When the doorbell rang, she stood up gracefully, her whole focus centered on serving Master Anderson well.

Opening the door, she bowed her head. "Welcome, Master Anderson."

"Hello, young Brie," he replied warmly. "Do you mind taking this bag from me?"

Brie glanced up to see he was holding a grocery bag out to her while juggling a ton of others with his other hand.

"Of course! I'd be happy to take more."

"One should do," he assured her, as he followed her inside. "I swear I've been to every corner of LA this morning getting the supplies I need."

She set his bag down on the counter. "You didn't need to go to all of that trouble."

"This is an important occasion," he stated, setting all his bags down. "I understand the significance of our scene today." Putting his hand over his heart, he told her, "I am honored that you chose me."

She bowed low at his feet. "I must thank you again for your help rescuing me, Master Anderson."

When he didn't say anything, Brie looked up and noticed he had tears in his eyes.

He quickly turned and swiped them away, saying in a gruff voice, "You may stand and serve your Master now."

Brie watched as he set a huge variety of fresh ingredients on the counter. He had also brought a small pillow and a bouquet of flowers.

She caught Shadow gliding down the stairs as if he were on the prowl. He snuck up to the kitchen, crouching low, his tail swishing back and forth.

"Don't think I don't see you there, blacky," Master

Anderson told the cat. "You can stare me down all you want." He waved around the chef's knife in his hand. "But, I'm the Master in this kitchen today."

Shadow seemed unimpressed by his declaration and glanced at Brie, blinking his yellow eyes slowly.

"I'm good," Brie told the cat with a grin.

Without looking back at Master Anderson, Shadow turned and walked down the hallway to the stairs.

"He's kind of become my watch-cat," she explained.

"Well, I can't hold that against the cuss," he replied with a wink.

"May I help, Master?" Brie asked.

"For now, you have only one duty."

"What's that?" she asked, eager to fulfill it.

Master Anderson turned to face her as he took off his cowboy hat and ripped off his shirt. Placing the hat back on his head, he flexed his chest muscles. "Admire your Master while he works his magic in the kitchen."

Brie immediately sat on a nearby barstool and rested her chin on her folded hands, happy to admire his fine body. "I remember being mesmerized by your cooking skills when I stayed with you in Denver."

"Those were good times, weren't they?"

She smiled and then giggled. "I'll never forget the fun we had with your neighbor."

Master Anderson threw back his head and laughed. "The look on her face when she caught us weeding—it was pure gold."

Brie couldn't stop grinning as she watched him work. He started the rice before slicing raw fish into impossibly thin and concise pieces. He was like a ballet artist in the way he moved about the kitchen, prepping for the scene.

Once all of it was assembled, he turned to her. "Are you ready, young Brie?"

She suddenly felt her nerves kick in as an image of kneeling before Holloway and eating out of his hand suddenly filled her mind.

"Take as much time as you need, darlin'," Master Anderson replied.

His warm voice helped to calm her. Brie understood if she was ever going to free herself of the shackles Holloway had placed in her mind, she had to take this first step toward her freedom.

Standing up, Brie bowed her head in respect. "I'm ready, Master."

"Do not be afraid to call out your safeword. I will not be offended. Triggers can happen at any moment, so you must acknowledge them whenever they crop up."

She glanced up at him, vowing, "I promise to call 'red' if I need to."

He clapped his hands together. "Excellent! Then I'm going to take a seat right here." Grabbing a kitchen chair, he turned it backward, swung a leg over it, and sat down to face her. With a wicked grin, he commanded, "Strip for your Master."

When Brie glanced at Sir's closed door, a sense of peace came over her. This objectification challenge was a charming way to begin the healing process. Nyotaimori was a beautiful art form that had nuances of bondage because she had to stay completely still while Master Anderson laid out the pieces of sushi and nigiri all over her body.

With graceful movements, Brie slowly undressed the way she had been taught at the Training Center. She teased him with glances of bare skin before letting the pieces of clothing fall to the floor. Once she was fully naked, she bowed her head. "Would you like me to turn, Master?"

"Of course."

Brie smiled while she slowly turned before him, blushing under Master Anderson's intense gaze. Sir had shaved her pussy earlier that morning—a sexy interlude in itself—so she could be a blank canvas for Master Anderson's creation.

Standing up, he held out his hand to her and commanded, "Come to me."

Brie walked to him, then squeaked when he swept her into his arms and laid her on the marble island. Goosebumps rose on her skin the moment she made contact with the cold stone.

"I brought this pretty pillow for your head," Master Anderson informed her, holding up a black silk pillow with a word stitched on it. "I prefer my exquisite platter to be comfortable."

Brie lifted her head, and he nestled the pillow under it. Master Anderson then began adjusting her limbs, laying her arms to her sides. He straightened her legs next, spreading them a little so her pussy was slightly exposed.

Studying her body intently, he appeared to be mapping out the design he planned to create. Once he was satisfied, he told her, "You know the drill. Pick a spot on the ceiling and don't move until I give you the command to."

"Yes, Master."

Brie stared up at the textured ceiling, finding a splotch that reminded her of a tiny violin. It brought her joy, and she was able to relax into the position she would have to hold for hours.

Master Anderson turned on the sound system, rocking the house with the deep, driving beat of dubstep. It took Brie back to the night the three of them had gone to the Beta Nightclub. Sir teased her mercilessly with the remote-controlled vibrator the entire evening, even while she danced with Master Anderson.

Although she kept her gaze obediently focused upward, Brie could see him out of the corner of her eyes. He was like a symphony conductor as he moved to the beat of the music, laying bamboo leaves over strategic areas on her body before filling them with the different sushi he had made. His touch was subtle, and Brie felt a thrill every time he added a new piece to her body.

As a finishing touch, Master Anderson cut the blossoms from the bouquet and placed them artfully on her body as floral accents, concentrating most of his effort between her legs.

When he was finished, Master Anderson turned off the music and stood back, stating proudly. "Damn, I think this is my best work yet!"

He got out his phone and hit record. Walking around her slowly, he spoke to the camera. "I call this art piece 'The Blooming Vagina.'"

Brie struggled not to laugh. The last thing she needed was for him to catch it in a video when she had fought so hard to remain still this entire time.

After he was done videoing her, Master Anderson placed the camera above her head and hit play so she could see it. Despite the humorous name he'd given her, he had truly transformed her body into a thing of beauty.

Brie was so touched that a lone tear escaped and slowly rolled down her cheek, unintentionally breaking the illusion of her being an inanimate object.

Master Anderson surprised her by quickly licking the tear away—and then snatched a piece of sushi from off her stomach.

"Perfect amount of salt to enhance the flavor," he stated, before popping it in his mouth. Because of his quick thinking, he'd saved her from the sting of failure.

She couldn't love Master Anderson any more than she did at that moment.

Grabbing another piece from the counter to replace the one he'd eaten, Master Anderson walked to Sir's office and rapped on the door. "Come admire my greatest achievement."

Brie heard Sir open the door. "Well, that certainly took longer than I expected."

Slapping his back. Master Anderson told him, "You can't hurry perfection, buddy."

The two men returned to the kitchen. Out of the corner of her eye, she saw Sir nodding as he looked her over. "I have to agree with you, Anderson. I have never seen such a stunning display in my life."

Being the focus of their admiration was exhilarating. Not wanting to distract from Master Anderson's work, Brie tried doubly hard to breathe slowly and keep her gaze trained on the tiny violin above her.

When Sir's stomach growled, Master Anderson handed him a pair of chopsticks. "The beauty of this art is that it's only temporary but leaves an indelible mark."

Brie felt goosebumps when Sir grazed her skin with the chopsticks as he took a piece from her thigh. Such a simple act, but he already had her body buzzing with a sensual current.

While the two men teased her with every bite they took, Master Anderson told Sir about his plans to propose to Shey. "She can't expect anything, buddy. I want it to be a complete surprise."

"Understood," Sir replied, taking a piece of nigiri that had been placed in the hollow of her throat. It sent delicious shivers through Brie.

"I had to case a few restaurants before I found one with a floor plan that allows you to take the photographs without being seen."

"You got permission from the owner, I hope." Sir chuckled. "The last thing I want is to be confronted as a stalker."

"I can just imagine it," Master Anderson said, grinning. "There you are, taking pictures of my grand proposal, and then you're dragged off by staff and kicked out of the restaurant. Wouldn't that be a hoot?" he laughed, slapping his thigh in amusement.

"Not for me," Sir replied drolly.

For the next hour, Brie listened with rapt attention as Master Anderson laid out every minute detail of his plan. It was over the top, but charming, and so totally Master Anderson.

Brie was certain Shey would love it!

After Master Anderson consumed the last bite, he commanded, "Eyes on me, young Brie."

She immediately gazed into his sparkling green eyes and squeaked as he swooped her off the counter and twirled her around, sending the leaves and flowers flying all over the kitchen.

He laughed as he set her down. "I couldn't resist."

Sir brushed the flower petals off his shoulder and smirked. "Did you enjoy the challenge, babygirl?"

Brie glanced at Master Anderson and smiled. "Very much so."

"Good."

Turning to Master Anderson, Sir asked, "Did you encounter any issues during the scene?"

Master Anderson beamed at Brie proudly. "She is brave and determined. A pleasure to scene with."

Brie bowed her head, thrilled to have completed her first challenge successfully.

Master Anderson handed her the pillow he had brought. "I want you to keep this in honor of today, young Brie."

When she took it from him, she was finally able to read the word stitched in gold thread:

THRIVE

Her bottom lip trembled, remembering Sir's promise to her. Crushing the pillow against her chest, she said with conviction, "I will, Master Anderson."

Brie looked at the pillow again, adopting that word as

her battle cry.

With Sir's guidance and the support of her found family, Brie was determined to do exactly that.

She would not only heal from the pain, but she would find a way to *thrive*.

Gentle Wolf

After the last reporter abandoned her in pursuit of better leads, Brie was grateful for the peace. Unfortunately, her reprieve did not last long.

The moment the authorities announced that a recently buried body had been discovered on the site of the compound, the press came back with a vengeance, hungry to know exactly what happened during Brie's captivity there.

There was nothing Sir could say or do to deter them this time. So, he installed soundproof inserts in the windows facing the street, telling Brie, "I will not allow them to impede our lives, and I resent that you and the children must be subjected to their constant invasion."

Brie was concerned, wondering what some of the other survivors might leak during their interviews. In the reporters' eagerness to unearth the atrocities Holloway had orchestrated, they were willfully ignoring the mental harm they could cause the survivors.

To the press, they were simply a "story" that had

proven too sensational not to pursue at any cost, regardless of the immense pain it would cause the victims and their families.

As for Brie, she had yet to tell her parents about her experience. It had been hard enough sharing it with Sir, knowing he would internalize it—her suffering becoming his suffering.

Thankfully, Sir was not a man who lived in a world of "what-ifs" and "if-onlys." He was actively pursuing a path to aid in her recovery and well-being.

Brie knew her parents would not be able to do the same. So, to protect herself as well as them, she had chosen to remain silent. But, that choice was stolen from her now that the press had broken down the defenses of several of the victims. Some of the reporters were zealously exploiting the horrors the survivors had suffered, hoping to further their careers by any means necessary.

When the public heard about sex slaves being tortured in the dungeon and the violent scenes the slaves were forced to play out, they went wild wanting to hear more. It was as if the world had some kind of sick fascination with it, needing to know every lurid detail while forgetting that real people had suffered.

Their morbid curiosity felt like a second assault to her.

Sir did his best to shield Brie from it, but he also warned her. "Whenever the press approaches you in public, ignore them. You mustn't react, no matter if they say something painful or incredibly far off-base. Give them nothing. Do not look at them, do not speak, and do not react. It's the only way to protect yourself, Brie. The second they find a crack, they will be relentless. Unfortunately, because you and Mary are known in Hollywood, you will be of particular interest to them."

She had already heard rumors that some members of the press were claiming she had been a willing participant in the macabre scenes, which was the reason behind her silence.

Even knowing that, Brie was caught unaware when her parents came to visit and her father confronted her on it. Holding a newspaper in his hand, he demanded, "Have you seen this? Is what they're saying true, little girl?"

Brie stared at the newspaper, shaking her head. "I don't know who 'they' are or what they're saying, Daddy. I avoid the news as much as possible."

"We suggest you do the same," Sir stated, standing beside Brie as he wrapped an arm around her protectively.

Her father turned on Sir. "I knew that asshole producer kidnapped my little girl, but what I read can't be true!" he insisted.

Then he looked at Brie helplessly, "Can it?"

She could barely breathe and was unable to answer.

Her father's hostile gaze returned to Sir. "If any of this is true, I blame you for what happened to my daughter. If you hadn't come into her life and polluted her mind with your perverse kinks, none of this would have happened!"

Brie felt chills when she heard her father's accusation, realizing it could rip her family apart.

Thankfully, Sir remained calm and stated firmly, "Don't believe everything you read in the newspaper."

"Please, Bill," her mother begged. "Can't we talk about this later? Look what it's doing to our daughter."

He waved his hand dismissively at his wife, telling her, "I have to know the truth, Marcy. I *need* to know what happened."

He then pointed at Brie, crying weakly, "That's my daughter for God's sake!" Her father broke into angry sobs, holding his hand up to his eyes as he tried to stop his tears.

Brie understood his anger came from a place of concern for her, but he was so consumed by it that he couldn't see that he was hurting her right now.

Rather than spell out what happened, she told him in a cold tone, "I was kidnapped and tortured, Daddy." She saw him flinch but continued. "I fought hard every day to survive so I could come back to my babies because I knew Thane would never give up until I was safe."

She glared at her father. "The only person responsible for what happened to me is Greg Holloway. If you don't understand that, then you have no place in my life."

It was as if an anvil had fallen, and the weight of her words echoed dangerously in the air.

Even as Brie said it, she was shocked by the words that had flown out of her mouth. However, she'd meant every word and refused to take them back.

Her father stared at her in stunned silence.

Brie knew she might be witnessing the death of her relationship with her father, but she could not—and would not—back down.

However, she was extremely resentful.

None of this would be happening if it weren't for the perverse lies being spread by the press—the very people who remained perched just outside her front door.

Not wanting Brie to be derailed by the strained relationship developing between him and her father, Sir set about creating her next challenge.

Brie found it curious that Sir chose Faelan to play out the encounter. There was a time when the two men had been fierce rivals.

Unable to accept Brie choosing Sir at the collaring ceremony, Faelan had tried to win her back by approaching her at the little shop where she worked. That encounter, along with her decision not to tell Sir about it, had led to her first punishment—with rice.

Sir's relationship with Faelan had changed significantly since then. So much so, that Sir now trusted him enough to scene with her.

Brie was anxious to see Todd Wallace in person because it was the only way she could tell whether he was doing okay. Although he'd returned from Russia to raise his baby daughter alone following the death of his wife, Brie was unsure how well he was handling the responsibility of parenthood or his grief.

While she waited for Faelan to arrive, Sir asked her, "Are you wondering about my choice of Dom?"

She smiled, still surprised that he could read her so well. "Maybe…"

Sir chuckled lightly. "I remembered when Wallace used the blindfold during your first scene together." Turning to her, he said, "I feel confident the familiarity you have with him will aid you significantly in this challenge. However, I also believe he may benefit from this encounter as well."

"That would make me happy, Sir."

Sir smiled, kissing her on the head. "I knew it would."

Concerned for Sir, she asked, "You're not uncomfortable with this arrangement?"

"Not at all. Are you afraid I might suffer feelings of jealousy?"

"Possibly," she answered, knowing his mother's actions had impacted Sir's ability to trust others.

Sir caressed her cheek as he gazed into her eyes. "The only way another man could steal your heart is if I have failed you in some way—and I will not fail you, babygirl.

"My condor," Brie murmured, standing on her tiptoes to kiss him.

"As with the last encounter, I will remain in my office unless you call for me." He started to walk away but then turned to address her. "One thing I want you to remember—Wallace is here to encourage your healing. I know you care about him, but his well-being is not your responsibility."

Brie nodded. "I appreciate the reminder, Sir."

She knelt in the foyer to prepare herself mentally before Faelan's arrival, but she was taken by surprise when he knocked on the backdoor before scooting inside.

"Davis advised me to avoid the front entrance because of the reporters," he explained, placing his tool bag on the floor.

Brie was surprised to see he was dressed in a dark blue business suit. It was stylish and formal, not casual like she was expecting.

She gazed into his blue eyes, struck by how authentic his false one was. If she hadn't known he'd lost it as gruesome payment for Rytsar's life, she would never have suspected the pain he'd endured at the hands of the Koslov brothers. She had come to admire his courage even more after all she had been through recently.

Brie bowed to him in respect. "Thank you for coming, Faelan."

"Before we begin, I think it's important you and I talk," he stated.

Her heart skipped a beat, concerned that Faelan might ask questions she was unwilling to answer.

"Sit beside me," he insisted, heading to the couch. He unbuttoned his jacket before sitting down. Smiling at her, he told her, "I am not going to pry, but I want to ask a few questions—as a friend."

Brie nodded, grateful he wanted them to speak as equals. She studied Faelan as she approached, noting that his cheeks were no longer hollow and the circles under his eyes not nearly as pronounced. She took it as a positive sign.

"How is your daughter?" she asked him.

Faelan actually grinned. "Kaylee is the sweetest baby.

So even-tempered and easy-going. She's all smiles." He shook his head. "I remember when all she did was scream. God, I couldn't handle all that crying. But I think…"

He paused for a moment, pain flitting across his face. "I believe she somehow sensed that her mother was dead, and her father had abandoned her."

Brie reached out to him. "You were simply grieving for your wife."

He frowned. "Kaylee couldn't know that, could she?" He sighed, "Anyway, today is about you, not me."

Switching gears, he asked, "How have you been adjusting?"

Brie met his ocean blue gaze, knowing he would understand on a level most could not. "I will never be the same."

He nodded in agreement.

"But, with Sir's guidance, I am learning to navigate the trauma I've experienced."

He snarled, "Thank God that place burned to the ground. Talk about hell on Earth."

Her stomach twisted into knots. "It was…"

Faelan put his arms around her. "You will be whole again, blossom. We both will."

She nodded, wanting to believe him. Neither Faelan nor she deserved the hands they'd been dealt in life. However, they were survivors, and they had a community that would stand beside them.

"Are you ready for today's session?" he asked quietly.

Brie was about to say yes, but she suddenly felt nervous.

"What has you spooked?"

"I asked to try the blindfold again, and Sir and I discussed it at great length. However, I would be lying if I told you I wasn't worried it might trigger me again."

"You are safe with me, blossom." He put his finger under her chin and looked into her eyes. "I want you to feel empowered by our session."

Brie nodded. "I want that, too."

Faelan took off his jacket and laughed when he saw the stain on his shirt. "Baby spit up," he explained.

"I think it makes you more attractive."

"I doubt most women would agree but thank you," he chuckled as he unbuttoned his shirt and cast it aside.

Faelan produced a long white feather and asked with a wolfish grin, "Are you ready to play, blossom?"

"I am, Faelan," she answered with growing confidence.

"First, you will undress, but I want you to leave your panties on."

Why she felt shy undressing in front of him when he had seen her naked many times before was a mystery to her. But his gentle gaze calmed her nerves.

Brie set her clothes in a neat pile and waited for his next command.

"Bow at my feet."

Brie felt butterflies, remembering their first encounter when he had surprised her with a blindfold, cuffs, and a large feather. She had secretly laughed at him, thinking they were such vanilla choices, but he had completely won her over by the end of their session.

For this scene, however, Brie had opted not to include the cuffs. She only felt comfortable testing her limits with the blindfold.

Faelan slipped off his shoes and socks, so he was left wearing only his dress pants. He still looked thin, his body reflecting the ravages of his grief, but he remained handsome with his blond hair and that easy grin.

Soon, however, his grin faltered, and Brie immediately picked up on his uneasiness. He chuckled uncomfortably, explaining. "This is the first time since…"

Brie looked at him with compassion. "We'll help each other through our scene."

He nodded, taking control again. "Lie with me, blossom."

Brie lay down on the floor beside Faelan. The smell of him was familiar and comforting.

Picking up the large feather, he asked, "Do you consent?"

She purred, drawn to its fluffy whiteness. "I do."

"Let's begin with your eyes open. Stay still."

Brie nodded and didn't move as Faelan guided the feather over her skin. The light touch of the feather caused her nipples to harden. It was exquisitely ticklish, making it difficult to remain still.

Faelan's grin returned. He knew the playful torment he was causing. When he felt she was ready, he commanded, "Now, I want you to close your eyes."

Brie readily obeyed, remembering how different the feather felt when she couldn't see it. It was as if the simple feather became an entirely new instrument.

She smiled when he ran it down the valley between

her breasts and tickled her stomach. It felt like hundreds of light touches teasing her skin all at the same time.

"You like that, blossom," he stated confidently.

She giggled. "I do, Faelan."

"Good." He took his time, teasing her body with the feather from the tip of her nose down to the sensitive underside of her toes.

Sensing she was enjoying it, he upped the challenge. Putting down the feather, he ordered, "Open your eyes."

Faelan held up a purple blindfold. "Do you consent?"

Her heart began to race when she saw the blindfold. "Yes."

"I want you to crave it, not fear it," he told her. "Therefore, I am going to begin by simply laying it over your eyes. Call out your safeword if it becomes too much."

Brie was astounded by Faelan's thoughtfulness. She had feared the moment he secured it behind her head. But Faelan was just as gentle with his re-introduction of the blindfold as he had been during their first encounter.

She smiled up at him. "Thank you, Faelan."

"My pleasure, blossom."

The instant Faelan laid the blindfold over her eyes, she smelled the scent of lavender. "I remember this…" she whispered, recalling the original blindfold.

"Lavender has the power to soothe the soul," he murmured huskily.

While she breathed in the calming scent, Faelan glided the feather over her skin. Her sensitivity to its touch now heightened, she began to crave the feel of it.

He grazed the feather along the swell of her hip. The tingling trail it left behind made her shiver in delight. Brie was able to lose herself in the simple stimulation, excited that she had experienced zero triggers.

When she felt ready, she told him, "I'd like you to secure the blindfold now."

Faelan removed the blindfold and smiled down at her. "Whatever happens next, I am proud of your courageous spirit, blossom."

Brie sat up so he could properly secure it. As soon as he tied it behind her head, she felt her anxiety begin to rise.

"Color?" he asked.

She tilted her head, trying to gauge her level of discomfort. Although her heart was racing as the same feeling of helplessness she'd experienced being locked in the dark cell took hold, Brie was still aware of her surroundings.

"A cautious yellow, Faelan," she answered truthfully.

"Would you like to continue?"

"Absolutely."

Faelan gently lowered her head to the floor, whispering, "You are in control."

Brie lay there for a moment, trying not to panic. She was afraid the dark melody would return. Instead, she became distracted by the hundreds of tickling points as Faelan grazed the feather over her breasts. He used the tip to tease her nipples, tickling them so much that she bit her bottom lip to keep from laughing.

"Now that I have your attention, I want you to concentrate on your pleasure."

He leisurely glided the feather over her stomach before making his way down her thighs and then all the way to her feet. The delicate touch drove her wild and she squirmed playfully as he tickled her toes.

Faelan abruptly stopped his artful torment, waiting a moment. Brie held her breath, wondering where he would touch her next.

Finally, he stroked the side of her face with the feather before grazing it over her lips, causing a delicious tingling.

That's when his warm lips pressed against hers. He gave her a tender kiss—not the kiss of a lover, but one of a cherished friend—and it filled her heart with immense joy.

"Can you handle one more challenge, blossom?"

"Yes," she answered enthusiastically.

"Do you remember my guessing game?

"Of course," Brie replied, remembering the day he'd won her at the auction and took her home to introduce her to his stimulating game.

"I only have one item today."

This game required a higher level of trust on her part. But, considering how careful he had been at planning out her scene today, Brie felt confident about playing the game.

"Do I have your consent?"

Brie nodded, but also answered verbally, "You do, Faelan."

"Perfect."

Brie held her breath, remembering their encounter during Kinky Eve when he had convinced her he was using a sharp knife on her skin when reality it had only been a feather.

"I want you to guess what this is," he commanded gently.

Goosebumps rose on her skin when she felt a cold, stiff pressure on her stomach. Her first guess was a piece of ice, but it seemed too thin. As Faelan dragged it across her skin, she thought her body heat might be changing its consistency. Then the familiar scent hit her nose, mixing nicely with the lavender she'd been smelling.

"Chocolate!" she exclaimed, smiling.

Chocolate held a special meaning for them. On the night of the auction, Faelan had introduced her to his chocolate "dance." It was a memory she still held dear.

"You are correct," Faelan answered. He then licked the trail of chocolate he'd made across her stomach.

Brie shivered in pleasure.

Faelan lifted the blindfold and grinned down at her. "Well done, blossom."

Brie could not express in words the feeling bursting inside her.

The song had not returned, despite the blindfold!

Wrapping her arms around his neck she pulled her head up and kissed him in gratitude. His lips tasted of milk chocolate.

"I'm so happy right now!" she gushed.

"Good," Faelan replied with satisfaction. "I would say this was a positive experience for both of us."

As they were redressing, Brie thought to mention, "One of our mutual friends saw you at the beach recently. Please feel free to visit us next time, if you want.

Our door is always open."

He shook his head. "While I appreciate the offer, our time at the beach is just for Kaylee and me."

Brie stopped what she was doing and looked at him with tenderness. "That's sweet."

He glanced sideways at her. "Don't tell anyone, but I visit the ocean once a week with my daughter so we can watch the sunset together. I swear, when I look out to the horizon at that magical moment just before the sun disappears, I can feel Kylie's presence."

Faelan looked at Brie with a wistful smile. "I hope Kaylee feels it, too."

Breath of Life

Still flying high after her successful scene with Faelan, Brie could not stop looking at Sir as they waited for his uncle to return with the children.

"Is there anything you would like to say?" Sir asked her when he caught her staring at him.

"You're a brilliant man, Mr. Davis."

He chuckled lightly.

"My scene with Faelan was exactly what I needed. But, he needed it as well."

"I knew it would be difficult for Wallace to embrace BDSM again without Kylie by his side. However, he is like you," Sir said with a knowing smile. "His Dominance is an essential part of his personality and will help him in the years to come."

Brie nodded, staring at Sir longingly.

Sir raised his eyebrow. "Is there anything else you would like to add?"

"I have a bad need to please, Sir."

He casually glanced down at his watch. "I estimate

we have fifteen minutes before Unc arrives."

"Plenty of time," she replied, feeling as if she might combust into flames if he said no.

Sir looked at her and barked, "Undress," while he unbuckled his belt.

Brie raced to get naked, her body humming with need.

Sir pushed her up against the wall, pressing his already rigid cock against her. She moaned with pleasure when he claimed her mouth with his.

She felt his hand slip between her legs, and he immediately pressed his finger into her pussy. "I see you are already wet, téa."

"So wet, Master…"

"I'm about to make you even wetter, my dear," Sir vowed as he began to pump her with his fingers.

Brie tilted her head back, craving his aggressive stimulation. However, she had to relax her body to fully give in to his demanding caress. Each thrust of his fingers sent electrical bursts of energy through her body. The feeling grew more intense with each thrust, driving her wild.

It didn't take long before the wet sound of her pussy filled the air, announcing her impending orgasm. Brie knew this was going to be a big one.

"Yes…" Sir growled, giving her permission.

Brie's entire body tensed, her inner muscles contracting tightly just before her release. "Oh, yes, yes, yes!" she screamed as her body shuddered from the strength of her climax.

Sir instantly knelt on the floor, burying his mouth in

her pussy. He greedily licked her watery come while he held her against the wall.

"So damn good…"

They were running out of time when Sir stood up and unzipped his pants. Grabbing the back of Brie's thighs, he lifted her, her back braced against the wall. Sir positioned his cock against her opening before plowing in.

Brie cried out in pleasure and relief as he started pumping her hard. But Sir needed more and tilted her hips so he could ram her even deeper.

The depth and angle of his thrusts stole all her thoughts away.

Digging his fingers into her thighs, he increased his thrusts, fucking her without restraint to the sounds of her passionate cries.

"More, more, more!"

When Sir came, he gritted his teeth, letting out a low groan as he released inside her. Brie held on to him with her legs wrapped tightly around his waist.

She loved the ferocity of their lovemaking. It was both powerful and raw!

Knowing that time was up, Sir set her back down. Brie stood there mutely, looking up at him in wonder as her entire body tingled with satisfaction.

Leaning one hand against the wall for support, he gave her a quick kiss while he caught his breath. "I'd say we have less than five minutes."

Brie quickly slipped her clothes back on. She was in the middle of pulling her skirt up when the doorbell rang.

Sir hastily grabbed a kitchen towel to clean up her watery excitement. "Go ahead and answer the door, babygirl," he said calmly as if they hadn't had the best quickie she'd ever experienced.

Still trembling from the mind-blowing sex, Brie opened the door and smiled when she heard Hope cry, "Mama!"

Taking Hope into her arms, Brie told Uncle Jack, "Thank you so much for watching the children for us." She turned to Judy who was holding Antony and added, "We appreciate it so much. Please come in!"

"We enjoy watching the children," Judy assured her. "It's a joy to see Jonathan playing with your kids. It's good for him to learn the importance of family at his age."

The moment they entered the house and Judy saw Sir cleaning the floor, she immediately said, "Oh, let me help you with that, Thane."

Sir chuckled good-naturedly as he finished wiping up the last of Brie's come. "No need, Auntie. Brie just spilled a little. It's nothing."

He glanced at Brie and gave her a private wink.

She instantly blushed and giggled as she turned away to rub noses with Hope. "Did you have fun with your cousin, sweet pea?"

Hope pointed to Jonathan excitedly. "Jon-Jon."

Brie set her down and Hope toddled up to him and hugged him around the neck. Brie grinned as she gazed at the little boy. Although he was full of boundless energy at age three, Jonathan had a tender way whenever he was near Hope. Brie could see his resemblance to

Lilly more clearly as time passed. It was reflected in the shape of his eyes, his mannerisms, and his engaging smile.

Although Lilly was the bane of Brie's existence, she refused to let it color her feelings toward the little boy. Jonathan was flourishing under Jack and Judy's loving care.

He deserved a future untainted by his lineage.

Based on the success of Brie's recent scene with Faelan, Sir felt comfortable with the timing of her next challenge. As for Brie, she was over the moon when she found out what was coming. She spent the day on pins and needles, impatient for her next scene to begin.

Unlike the sessions before, Sir insisted on leaving Brie alone, choosing to take the children with him to visit her parents instead. "I'm concerned that my presence could hinder the scene. Besides, the tension between your father and I must be resolved and I am certain I can reason with him."

Brie frowned, looking at him with sympathy. She knew how stubborn her father could be. "I wish you luck, Sir."

Before leaving the house with the kids, Sir turned to face her and said tenderly, "I know you, babygirl. You always race forward, hungry to conquer the next thing that stands in your way. But healing takes time. Be patient with yourself today."

She chuckled softly. "I will try, Sir."

He raised an eyebrow.

She immediately corrected herself. "I *will*, Sir."

"Much better," he said, kissing her on the forehead.

Brie hugged both of their children and then gave Sir a good luck kiss before they left.

She was struck by how empty the house felt once they were gone and sighed loudly. She looked down when Shadow pressed his cheek against her leg. "It's just you and me, kid."

She knelt on the floor in the middle of the living room, and Shadow immediately crawled into her lap. Brie stilled her mind as she listened to the cat's low, rumbling purr. It was so peaceful and calming that she was startled when she heard the light rap on the back door.

Brie opened her eyes and grinned when she saw Tono through the glass of the door. Shadow leaped out of her lap and ran to it.

She stood up gracefully before hurrying to let him in. His long, dark bangs partially covered those chocolate brown eyes. That, combined with his gentle smile, still had the power to give her butterflies.

"Tono!" she cried as she opened the door wide and invited him inside.

"I am grateful to see you." The tone of his voice instantly soothed her soul. Tono casually set his tool bag down and held out his arms to her.

Brie pressed her head against Tono's chest, closing her eyes as she hugged him. It felt as if her soul had suddenly gotten its breath back. "I'm so glad you're here."

He pulled back and looked at her tenderly, brushing a strand of her hair from her cheek. In a voice full of gratitude, he stated, "I welcome in this moment with you."

She looked at him curiously.

Meeting her questioning gaze, he told her, "I was unsure if it would be given to me."

The pain of everything she'd suffered suddenly came back in waves. In a shaking voice, Brie confessed, "I wasn't sure either."

He gently cradled her face in both of his hands, his deep brown eyes absorbing her pain. "I felt the depth of your suffering as if it were my own, toriko."

"I felt our connection, Tono." She hesitated before continuing. "It strengthened me when I had nothing left."

His gaze intensified. "I refused to stop meditating until I heard your voice on the phone."

She shook her head in disbelief. "I wasn't rescued for eight days."

Tono nodded. "Autumn provided me with continuous nourishment so I could remain focused on you." He grazed her cheek with his hand. "I made a vow not to break the connection until you were safe."

Her bottom lip trembled. "I was so scared…"

"I know."

She looked at him sorrowfully, knowing he had felt the pain of her suffering.

As if Tono could read her thoughts, he told her, "I was honored to share your pain, toriko." His gentle smile moved her. "And I would do so again without hesitation because I am unwilling to face a world without you in it."

Brie laid her head back on his chest and closed her eyes, forcing back all the fear and uncertainty she'd endured, as she concentrated on the steady beat of his heart.

Shadow had been constantly rubbing against Tono's legs the entire time. Tired of being ignored, he finally let out a loud meow.

Tono looked down at the car, stating solemnly, "Thank you, Shadow. You have done well."

"He's been watching over the children at night and over me during the day."

Tono reached down to pet Shadow. "You are a warrior for this family."

"Yes," Brie agreed as she studied Tono more closely. Still recovering from the kidney disease that almost took his life, Tono looked healthier than the last time she'd seen him, but she felt he was still suffering on an emotional level. "Are you okay?"

"I am content," he said, meeting her gaze. When she gave him a doubtful look, he assured her, "I have everything I need—truly."

Glancing at his tool bag, Tono told her, "I look forward to our session together."

Brie instantly smiled, longing for the feel of his rope. "I do, too."

Before starting the session, she asked him, "Would you like me to make some tea before we begin?"

Tono shook his head, chuckling lightly. "Let's wait to savor it after we're done. I anticipate that this will be a long session."

Brie blushed, remembering when she'd interrupted their first rope scene together because she needed to pee. Although she later found out that it had been part of Tono's lesson that day, she preferred not to repeat it.

While Tono rolled out his jute mat in the center of the room, Brie asked, "Would you rather do it outside like we did last time?"

He shook his head. "No, toriko. We cannot afford any distractions."

Although she was curious as to why, Brie did not question his reasoning.

Tono then handed Brie a wrapped gift. "Get dressed and meet me out here when you are ready."

Brie smiled at him graciously. "You didn't have to get me a gift."

"It was my pleasure to do so."

Brie headed into the bedroom, admiring the box he had meticulously wrapped in white paper and jute twine. She unwrapped it with reverence and lifted out a white silk kimono with artfully placed branches of cherry blossoms.

The beauty of the simple design stirred her on a soul level.

Brie quickly undressed so she could wrap herself in the soft silk. Running to the mirror, she tied the obi around her waist the way Tono had taught her. She took a moment to stand back and admire the beautiful kimono.

The brilliant white of the silk suggested purity, and the cherry blossoms held special meaning for her. She heard Tono's voice in her head when he'd explained: *"The cherry blossom represents renewal and hope."*

Staring at herself, Brie slowly turned in front of the mirror. Although she would never be the same after what she'd endured, Brie knew she had the power to reclaim the things she held most dear.

No one could steal that from her—not even Holloway.

When Brie returned, Tono took one look at her and murmured in admiration, "*Utsukushii.*"

The look of respect in his eyes touched her deeply.

Brie noticed that he had changed into his black kimono while she was gone. It made him look even more distinguished and handsome. Gesturing to the mat, he commanded, "Come, toriko."

Brie glided across the floor, inexplicably drawn to him. She knelt on the mat and waited as he turned on the soothing music of a lone flute.

"This will be a long process, toriko," he reminded her.

Brie nodded and held her breath as he knelt behind her. The moment she felt his arms wrap around her as he pressed her body against his chest, she finally let out her breath.

"Breathe with me, toriko," he whispered softly in her ear.

Although she had been looking forward to this, she suddenly found the restraint of his arms frightening. The memories it evoked made it difficult for her to match his breath.

Tono did not loosen his hold, forcing her to concentrate on him. "Find my breath."

Brie swallowed back her fear and took slow, deep breaths, trying to sync her breathing with his. What had always been a natural process for her was now frustratingly difficult. Shaking her head, she finally cried out in disappointment, "I can't."

"You can," he replied with quiet strength.

Brie closed her eyes. But, instead of actively trying to match his breath, she slowed down her rapid breathing. After several minutes, she felt herself naturally syncing with his.

The moment the connection was made, her muscles began to relax. It wasn't long before she stopped resisting his tight embrace and they breathed in unison.

"Very good," he murmured gently. "If you start to feel anxious again, I want you to match your breath to mine."

Brie nodded.

In a soothing voice, Tono explained, "If it becomes too much at any point, call out your safeword and we will start at the beginning…as many times as you need." She could hear the smile in his voice when he added, "We have all the time in the world, toriko."

His words lifted her spirits.

Tono released her to pick up a bundle of rope. He showed it to her, stating, "I promise that today I will transport you to nirvana with my jute."

"May I smell it?"

He held it up to her nose and Brie breathed in its earthy smell, savoring it.

Tono opened her kimono slightly, exposing her

cleavage. "My rope's caress is an expression of my profound love for you, toriko," he stated. "I have no wish to harm you."

"I know, Tono." She smiled, sighing in contentment. "I love the feel of your rope."

"Remember that," he replied gently before asking, "Which decorative bondage would you like to begin with?"

"The very first one we did together." She turned her head, grinning at him. "I remember it felt like a tight hug."

"The Japanese Pearl Harness," he stated, smiling as he gently grasped her arms and lifted them above her head. "Keep your arms up, toriko."

With artistic precision, Tono slowly began to wrap the jute around her chest, crisscrossing it above and below her breasts. Brie enjoyed the binding because of how beautiful it made her breasts look when they were framed by his rope.

But, as he went about the process of binding her, Brie was caught off guard. Instead of the rope's tight restriction bringing her comfort, she suddenly felt queasy and unsettled.

Before she had a chance to voice those feelings out loud, Tono intuitively stopped and asked, "What is wrong?"

She burst into tears. "I don't know, Tono. I don't want to call my safeword, but I feel scared right now." She turned her head to look at him. "How is that possible when I'm with you?"

He gave her a sympathetic smile. "I may be able to

explain it," he replied as he loosened the rope with quick movements and laid the jute down beside her.

Gathering Brie in his arms, Tono rocked her slowly as he spoke. "It is natural that you might associate me with the torture you endured. Although our connection helped provide you with comfort, it is now intertwined with that experience. Since you were held against your will, anything that triggers the feeling of not being in control has the potential to set off your fear."

Shaking her head violently, Brie shouted in anger, "I don't want our connection to be stolen from me—or my love of the jute!"

Tono held her tighter. "Which is why I am here with you, toriko. I will repeat the binding process as many times as needed. This is not something you can force. It must be done with gentle persistence."

Brie leaned her back against him and sighed miserably. "I think I understand now. Even though I hate it, I will not be able to submit to you fully until I submit to each stage of this process."

"Yes, that is a healthy way to think of it," Tono told her. "Be patient with yourself during this session. You and I? We have all the time in the world."

Brie nodded and closed her eyes, once more syncing her breath with his.

"We will start with a much simpler form of bondage," Tono suggested.

She knew exactly which one she wanted. "Let's do the warrior cuff."

"An excellent way to begin," he agreed.

Tono spent the day walking Brie through ever more

complicated bondage techniques and designs. It disturbed Brie that she felt nothing inside—as if the joy she once felt for the rope was gone.

To make matters worse, Brie had to call her safeword several times. Each time she did, Tono would quickly unbind her, and then they would start by syncing their breaths again.

Tono's infinite patience and encouragement helped Brie finally get to the point where she wanted to give the Japanese Pearl Harness another try.

He nodded and ordered gently, "Lift your arms, toriko."

Brie closed her eyes, smiling when he reminded her, "We are all in harmony. You, me…the rope."

She was acutely aware of how the tightness of the rope restricted her breathing once her chest was fully bound.

"Feel the restriction and embrace it," Tono encouraged her.

Rather than let fear overtake her, Brie calmed her quick, shallow breaths to match Tono's controlled breathing.

The strength of their connection caused her to purr in genuine contentment.

"Give me your wrist," Tono commanded. When she held it out to him, he lightly grasped it and placed it behind her back. Brie enjoyed the tug and pull of the rope as he secured her wrist to the intricate ties he'd already created.

He then asked Brie to hold out her other wrist. She did so without hesitation. Tono praised her and began the intricate lacing between both arms. Brie felt the power of his rope as Tono slid the jute over her skin, teasing her with its alluring touch.

To her surprise and delight, Brie began to lose herself to the call of the rope.

Tono noticed the tear running down her cheek and stopped. "Talk to me, toriko."

Brie opened her eyes, whispering, "I'm starting to fly, Tono."

He smiled, turning her head to kiss her on the lips before resuming his work. "Enjoy nirvana, toriko. You have earned it."

Musketeers

The light of the sun filtering through the window woke Brie, and she was surprised to find herself in bed with Sir. She had no memory of what happened after she drifted into subspace with Tono, but she could still feel the glorious remnants of that high.

Smiling, she turned slowly in the bed to look at Sir. Whenever she caught him sleeping, his relaxed expression had a boyish look to it—but not this morning. She could see lines of concern on his forehead, and his lips were flattened into a tense line.

Even in sleep, he could not find any rest or escape.

Brie was worried for him. She understood the pressure he was under. Sir was determined to help her heal while watching over the kids and continuing to work. All of it was taking a heavy toll on him.

She attempted to slip out of bed unnoticed so he could sleep in, but the moment her foot touched the floor she heard him ask, "Did you sleep well?"

"I did, Sir," she answered, turning to him. "But I

didn't mean to wake you."

He sat up in bed. "I wasn't sleeping well anyway."

She looked at him with concern. "How are you doing, Sir?"

He failed to answer her. After a few tense seconds, however, his eyes softened. "I was happy to come home and hear you had a breakthrough with Nosaka. I haven't seen you fly that high in a long time, babygirl."

Brie thought back to yesterday and shivered. "I was shocked when I felt nothing at first. But Tono was able to explain why, and he never wavered in his confidence that I would experience flight again."

She crinkled her brow. "What happened to Tono?"

He chuckled. "Nosaka stayed several hours after I returned home, and we talked while he attended to your aftercare. He's currently on a plane headed home as we speak."

Brie frowned. "I'm sad I didn't get the chance to thank him."

Sir smiled, reaching out to graze her jaw with his thumb. "Trust me. Seeing you in subspace was the only thanks he wanted."

Brie tilted her head, turning her attention back on Sir. "How did it go with my parents?"

His hesitancy to answer her question spoke volumes.

Looking at him with sympathy, she said, "I feel guilty for enjoying myself when you were stuck dealing with my unreasonable father."

"Guilt has no place here, babygirl. I chose to speak with him."

"But my parents are needlessly causing you stress."

Sir shook his head. "You mean *our* parents. Bill and Marcy accepted me into the family with open arms, and a disagreement between us doesn't change that."

Brie growled. "I hate that my dad is being such an asshole to you!"

Sir held up his hand to stop her. "I don't want to hear you speaking about your father in that way. He may be overbearing and hardheaded, but he loves you. You should reserve those words for people who hurt you with deliberate malice."

She realized he was talking about his mother and half-sister, and it gutted her. Sir deserved only the best from others. Unfortunately, he had experienced the worst—from members of his own family.

Brie looked at him with admiration. "If my father truly understood what an exceptional person you are, he would bow at your feet."

Sir laughed uncomfortably and smirked. "That is something I hope I never see."

Brie was excited when Lea called and invited her to hang out at her place. When she arrived, she was pleasantly surprised to learn that Mary would be joining them.

"How the heck did you convince her to come?"

Lea grinned. "I told you Mary can't resist my jokes. Although she claims she never read a single one that I sent, I know her. Mary's a closet Lea fan, no doubt about it."

Brie laughed. "Whether she secretly loves your jokes or not, what you did made a real difference to her. Thanks for being you, girlfriend."

Lea shrugged. "Mary and I may have a past that hasn't always been pretty, but she's the real deal, snarky attitude and all."

Brie nodded in agreement.

When the doorbell rang, Lea insisted on answering the door herself. Brie's jaw dropped the second Mary walked into the apartment. She had cut off her long blonde hair and now wore a short bob.

Mary narrowed her eyes. "What the hell are you two gawking at?"

Lea shrugged. "Just taking in the new you."

Mary rolled her eyes. "I'm the same fucking bitch, so you two cunts can look the other way."

Brie thought the hairstyle was flattering on Mary's face and told her, "It complements you."

"Like I give a damn," Mary snorted in disgust. "I just needed a change."

Lea's eyes flashed with excitement, seeing an opportunity for a joke. "What did one curly hair say to the other curly hair when they asked for a dance?"

Mary shook her finger at Lea. "Don't you even—"

When Lea opened her mouth, Mary immediately stopped her. "Zip it, big boobs. I'm warning you."

"But—"

"I'm serious," she snarled.

"You haven't even heard the—"

Mary glanced at the door. "You want me to leave right now?"

Lea pouted her bottom lip and looked at Brie helplessly.

Brie gave Lea a sympathetic smile and shrugged, knowing Mary wouldn't budge. "You heard the lady."

Poor Lea looked like she was ready to burst from having to hold in the punchline. Somehow, though, she managed and squeaked, "Anyone want something to drink?"

"I'll have the usual," Mary replied, sitting down.

Lea turned to Brie and asked in the same high-pitched voice, "And you, Stinky Cheese?"

"I'll have whatever you're having."

Lea closed her eyes in pain, muttering, "I have the perfect joke for that…"

"But you're going to keep it to yourself so we can actually enjoy ourselves for a change," Mary insisted.

Lea sighed and turned without further protest, heading to her kitchenette.

Brie glanced at Mary. "She just wants to make you laugh."

Mary shook her head. "If I give Lea an inch, she'll take a mile. She never stops yapping. She's like a little Chihuahua." Holding up her hand, she moved it like a hand puppet. "Yap, yap, yap…"

Lea walked back with their drinks, biting her lip to keep from talking.

Mary took the drink and held it up. "Thank God for Captain. He's the only man I'll let fuck me these days."

Brie and Lea both looked at each other, taken aback.

Mary raised an eyebrow. "Get your minds out of the gutter, bitches. I'm talking about Captain Morgan." With that, Mary downed the drink in no time flat. "Hit me with another."

Lea crossed her arms. "Only if you let me finish my joke."

Mary glanced at the empty glass and huffed. "I'll pass."

Thankfully, Mary's quick consumption of the rum and Coke seemed to mellow her out. From the moment she'd stepped into the apartment, she'd seemed to be on edge. Although Brie couldn't blame her after everything she'd suffered, she hoped Mary understood she was with friends, and that this was a safe place.

Lea remained silent, sipping at her fruity drink while Brie talked openly about some of the things she'd experienced at the compound. Eventually, she went on to detail the steps Sir was taking to help her work through her trauma.

Mary said nothing but continued to nod as Brie spoke. It seemed Mary was distracted, as if her thoughts were elsewhere.

"What's on your mind, Mary?" Brie finally asked her.

"I can't stop thinking about the baby…" Her voice caught when she added, "They found his mother's remains buried in the woods not far from the compound."

"I remember when they reported about that," Lea whimpered. "It's so awful."

Brie hated that the young woman died just days before they were rescued. It was so unfair.

She asked Mary softly, "Did you know her?"

"None of us *knew* each other. That was part of

Greg's strategy. It ensured his slaves remained passive and weak. But, I did see her in passing many times while I was there, and I was worried about her."

Brie stared at Mary in horror. "You've been to the compound before?"

Mary's eyes darkened. "He took me there whenever he needed to 'correct' me."

Hearing Mary's dark secret, Brie felt suddenly sick. "Why didn't you tell me?"

"Greg said he would kill them all if I ever breathed a word about it." Mary frowned and then became silent, a haunted look darkening her eyes. "…I've been tormented with guilt ever since."

Brie shuddered, knowing Holloway had used that same tactic on her. She looked at Mary with profound sorrow. "Oh, Mary…"

"Don't!" she snapped. "The last thing I want is anyone's sympathy—especially you."

The three of them sat there in uncomfortable silence for several minutes.

"I can't stop thinking about that kid," Mary finally spoke up, glancing at the two of them. "No one's stepped up to claim him." Shaking her head, she growled. "It's not right!"

Brie immediately thought of Antony, her mother's heart imagining her son lost and alone in the world because no one wanted him. It crushed her.

"Hasn't any family come forward?" Lea asked.

Mary's frown deepened. "No, and it pisses me off! If he was a puppy, people would be clamoring to take him, but because he's a child born into this perverse situation, people don't want anything to do with the kid."

Brie was moved when she saw tears in Mary's eyes when she choked out, "It's like the world blames this little kid for what Greg did when he's just a baby for Christ's sake!"

Mary lowered her head as the tears continued to fall. "He deserves to be loved."

Brie wondered if Mary identified with the child and wanted him to have the future she never had.

Lea spoke up. "Have you looked into adopting him?"

Mary swiped away her tears, rolling her eyes at Lea. "No one is going to allow a single woman to adopt a baby."

"You'd be surprised," Lea informed her. "It happens more often than you think. You'd make a great parent, Mary. As long as you lose your snarky attitude, get some parental counseling, and laugh a heck of a lot more."

Mary stuck her tongue out at Lea.

"You know what they say—it takes two to tangle."

Looking at Lea as if she were an idiot, Mary demanded, "What the fuck are you talking about?"

"That's the joke," Lea answered gleefully. "Two curly hairs that want to dance…"

Mary threw up her arms in exasperation. "Get me another drink, you freak!"

Lea winked at Brie as she headed back to the kitchen to refresh everyone's drink.

When she returned, Brie brought up something that had been eating at her. "I haven't spoken to Darius yet." Taking a sip of the fruity drink to calm her nerves, she added, "I haven't been brave enough to."

Lea looked at her with compassion. "It must be hard, considering your history with the guy."

Brie nodded, the weight of it wearing on her soul. "I can't forget how cruel Darius was to me growing up, and it's hard for me to reconcile who he was with the man he is today."

She looked at both of her friends in desperation. "I know if it weren't for him, I would not be here right now. I owe him my life."

Taking another sip of the drink, Brie swallowed down the memories of him assaulting her as a child, and stated matter-of-factly, "He risked everything by ratting out Holloway, but…I can't forget the smug look on his face when he saw me at the compound."

Mary spoke up. "Trust me. If he had acted any other way, Holloway would have noticed. I guarantee he did it out of self-preservation."

Brie nodded, accepting the truth of Mary's statement. "I need to thank Darius. I know that. He's a hero. Not only did he save my life, but he saved everyone who was in the compound that night."

"I wouldn't say anything," Mary said, surprising her. "If word gets out and Holloway discovers who the rat is, Darius may still pay."

Brie froze, suddenly stricken.

Lea reached out and squeezed her hand. "Stop worrying about everyone else, Stinky Cheese. Right now, you need to concentrate on taking care of yourself."

Giving Mary the side-eye, Lea added, "Do you know why the blonde with the bob stared at the orange juice bottle for two hours?" Before Mary could stop her, Lea blurted, "Because it said *concentrate.*"

Brie burst out laughing while Mary glared at Lea, speechless.

It was wonderful knowing that the three musketeers were still alive and well.

Kitten

Sir discussed the next session at length with Brie. "It may prove the most challenging yet."

Brie couldn't imagine anything more challenging than her scene with Tono. If it hadn't been for his extraordinary patience, she never would have entered subspace bound in his jute.

"Why do you feel that way, Sir?" she asked in concern.

"Two reasons, really. It will take place in a different environment. Although I will be in a nearby room, the unfamiliar surroundings will still be an adjustment for you. Also, Baron will be asking you to give up a higher level of control."

Brie smiled in relief when she heard who her Dom would be for the session. "I trust Baron completely, Sir."

"As do I, which is why I wanted him to partner with you tonight. I can't think of a person better qualified to work with you on this. Baron's experience with subs who have suffered trauma, along with your history of training with him at the Center, makes him the perfect candidate."

"I wholeheartedly agree."

Sir gazed deep into her eyes. "It will be extremely important that you honor your safeword, babygirl."

Brie chuckled lightly. "Trust me. Tono taught me that, repeatedly."

Sir nodded. "Still, I cannot emphasize it enough."

Brie put her arms around Sir. "I have to admit, I'm looking forward to this session. Scening in a different location makes me feel like I'm starting to piece my life back together. I'm determined not to let Holloway have any part of me."

Sir took her hand and kissed it. "Téa, my invincible goddess."

As Sir pulled up to Baron's home, he explained, "I will remain upstairs with Captain and Candy. They are having their weekly discussion group with their current class of students, and they felt I might benefit from listening in. If you need me at any point, let Baron know. There is no reason for you to suffer, not even for a second."

"I appreciate that, Sir."

Walking up to the house, Brie found herself brimming with confidence. It wasn't just that she'd scened with Baron before. She'd also taught a lesson here with Sir and had fond memories of this place.

With Baron as her Dom, she knew she was in safe

hands. She was thrilled when he answered the door to greet them. "Welcome, Mr. and Mrs. Davis, my honored guests."

Baron moved to the side to let them in. He gestured for Sir to join the group in the main room and asked Brie, "Would you like anything to eat or drink before we begin our session?"

She shook her head, laughing. "Based on the length of my last session, I think I should wait before drinking anything."

"Duly noted," he said with a wink, leading her down the hallway. "How are you feeling about tonight's scene?"

Brie stopped for a moment and faced him. "To be honest, I'm really excited, Baron. After my breakthrough with Tono, I feel optimistic about this challenge with you."

"Good," he replied with a relaxed smile as he pointed her toward the spiral staircase leading to the basement.

Brie headed down it, her heart light. She glanced at the inviting sign above the doorway that read "The Power Exchange."

"Baron, more than ever, I appreciate this name."

He glanced up at the sign and stated, "A submissive's power is never stolen in my play space."

When Brie walked into the large area, she was struck again by the elegance of the environment. She looked at the antique St. Andrew's Cross, the sumptuously padded spanking benches, and the intricately carved wooden stockades. Every piece matched the beauty of the

Roman-inspired mosaic on the wall.

But, when Brie noticed the golden chains on the whipping poles and the decorative cages at the far end of the expansive room, she felt the first telltale signs of discomfort.

Although they were beautiful, her mind snapped back to the horrors of the compound, and she shivered unconsciously.

Baron noticed her staring at them. "You are safe here, kitten. I will keep reminding you of that throughout our session together."

Brie nodded, trying to quell the uneasiness she felt as she scanned the room again. It was shocking how different she felt standing here looking at all the items on display. When Baron had first shown her his secret play area, she had loved everything about it. Perspective changed everything.

This is a safe space, Brie reminded herself.

"As you know, I plan to use the sex swing tonight, but I am open to doing something different if you prefer."

She smiled, appreciating his offer. "No, Baron. I'm looking forward to it. Truly."

Baron nodded. "You're in charge tonight. However, if there comes a point when I feel we should stop, I will end our session myself."

Brie placed her hand on his. "I trust you."

"I value that more than you know, kitten."

She gazed at him with a heart full of gratitude. "You've been supportive of me from our very first scene together at the Training Center. And you came to my rescue when I was at the Kinky Goat. You have *earned* my trust many times over, Baron."

He gently cupped her chin with his large hand. "I want you to lean into that trust tonight."

When Baron pressed his full lips against her mouth, Brie closed her eyes, drawing strength from his gentle kiss.

Pulling away, he commanded, "Strip for me, kitten. I leave it up to you how much you take off."

Baron's decision allowing her to choose how much skin she wanted to bare certainly created a different dynamic for Brie. However, she was determined to match the same level of submission she'd experienced her first time scening with him.

As she stripped, Brie purposely kept her gaze on him while she slowly removed each piece of clothing. She knew that the process of undressing was an important part of a scene—but tonight, that was doubly true.

For Brie, this was her declaration of freedom from Holloway and the damage he had inflicted on her.

"Beautiful," Baron murmured when she stood before him completely naked.

Brie lowered her eyes, smiling inside and out. "Thank you, Baron."

"Do you consent?" he asked in a husky voice, nodding toward the dark purple swing with gold hand-and-foot holds hanging in the air.

"I do, Baron. Very much so."

Lifting her off the ground, Baron carried her in his muscular arms to the swing. Before placing her in it, he looked down at her intently. She could see his concern for her in his hazel eyes.

Kissing her again, Baron infused her with his masculine energy.

Setting Brie into the swing, he helped guide her feet into the hanging stirrups while she grabbed the hand supports. Having her legs spread and her pussy splayed definitely made her feel exposed and vulnerable, but she wanted to relive the full experience of their first scene.

She was caught off guard the moment Baron let go and she started to swing in midair. Brie suddenly panicked. She felt completely out of control as she swayed above the ground, and she struggled in the harness.

Whimpering in fear, she cried out for Baron.

"Shh…" he replied calmly, immediately returning to her and holding the swing still. Even though her heart was still racing, Brie was comforted by his presence and began to relax.

"What happened?" he asked.

"The swing is definitely a trigger for me," she admitted. "Swaying helplessly in midair intensifies feeling out of control for me. But…" She looked up at him in surprise. "…I think it was the separation from you that set it off. As soon as you let go, I was completely unraveled."

It was something of a relief to Brie. She was happy it wasn't submitting to Baron that she feared, but the loss of connection with him.

"I have a solution for that," he stated confidently. "I want you to kiss me as I let go of the swing."

Brie nodded even though she felt fearful butterflies in her stomach. When Baron let go and she started to swing weightlessly in the air, she lifted her head. The instant their lips connected, she felt grounded again.

"Yes…" she murmured when he broke the kiss.

"Whenever you need that connection, I want you to kiss me."

She smiled. "It would be my pleasure, Baron."

He was creative, using the potency of his touch, the magic of his kisses, and a variety of sensation tools to build her confidence step by step. When he felt she was finally ready, he told her, "I'm going to make you orgasm while you swing in the air."

Her eyes widened. The idea both excited and frightened her. "I'm not sure I can climax," she told him shyly.

"Do you remember the gel?" he asked with a sexy smirk.

Brie grinned, remembering the sensual heat caused by the gel he had used during one of their first scenes. It was potent enough that it had gotten her overly excited.

"Unlike the last time, you are allowed to come. In fact, I command it," he replied with a low, inviting growl. "But first, I want to caress this beautiful body of yours."

Brie watched as he ran his dark hands over her body. She delighted in their different skin tones because it made for a striking contrast.

She bit her lip when Baron reached between her legs and lightly rubbed her pussy before applying the gel. She instantly felt the heat begin to build as he spread the watery gel over her clit and outer lips.

After wiping his hands clean, Baron went back to gliding them over her body, concentrating on her shoulders, breasts, and stomach.

The gel made her clit super sensitive, causing her to gasp in surprise and pleasure whenever he used the lightest of touches on her clit. In no time, Baron had her squirming in the swing with desire.

Brie's eyes widened when he took out a bullet vibrator. "Do you consent, kitten?"

She nodded, moaning with excitement just thinking about the bullet touching her clit.

Baron turned it on, filling the room with the buzz of the small instrument. Holding on to the swing, he kept her still while he pressed the bullet against the side of her clit. Goosebumps rose on her skin as her body responded to the sensual vibration making her pussy extremely wet.

Baron let go of the swing while still pressing the bullet against her. The brief sway unsettled Brie, but for some reason that slight feeling of loss of control seemed to excite her.

Taking hold of the swing again, Baron removed the vibrator and smiled down at her. "When I release the swing again, I want you to adjust to the feeling of freedom.

Freedom…

It suddenly struck Brie that she was interpreting the feeling of leaving the ground as being out of control when before she'd embraced it as a form of freedom. Of flight…

She'd just experienced another breakthrough, realizing that it was the same association she'd made with being blindfolded and being tied in Tono's jute.

Having the power to change that misaligned perspective was life-affirming for Brie.

She gazed into Baron's hazel eyes and voiced her deepest desire, "I long to feel that freedom again."

"I know, kitten," he murmured.

Baron let go of the swing, allowing it to sway slightly as he used the bullet to play with her clit. Brie's nipples hardened as her climax began to build.

Her excitement was laced with a tinge of fear, but she'd decided that facing that challenge head-on was exactly what she needed.

It took time for her to fully let go but, as soon as she did, her thighs began to shake. Baron leaned down and whispered gruffly, "Come for me, kitten."

Brie threw her head back, embracing the thrill of her impending orgasm, coupled with the swaying movements of the swing.

She cried out in victory as the rush of her orgasm overtook her.

Baron then gave the swing an extra push so that she swayed effortlessly above the air as her body shuddered in ecstasy.

The feeling was glorious, making her laugh with pure joy!

Baron took extra time with his aftercare, praising Brie for her courage. She was riding on such a high that she felt like a heavyweight champion who'd just crushed her opponent in the ring…

…then her eyes drifted to the golden handcuffs hanging from the whipping pole.

She was instantly taken back to her dark cell, where she was bound in handcuffs, waiting for Holloway to return.

It sent her spiraling down a dark hole.

What if her victory today was just an illusion and she would never know true freedom?

She murmured out loud, "I'm not brave."

"You are braver than you know, kitten," Baron insisted in a commanding tone. He kissed her hard, sealing his decree.

Afterward, when Baron led her back upstairs, Brie was surprised to find the other subs were waiting for her. These women and men had all been hurt by abusive people masquerading as Dominants. They were fighting to reclaim their submission just as she was.

Only they could truly understand the battle she'd just fought, so it broke her heart in the most beautiful way when they encircled her in silent solidarity and put their hands on her, wanting to celebrate her victory.

Although it felt small to Brie, their heartfelt observance reminded her that tonight had been an important step toward her freedom.

Brie looked sheepishly at Sir on the drive home. "You are right about me."

"How so?" he asked, glancing at her with interest.

"I've been in such a rush to conquer my fears that I've been losing sight of the small victories. Tonight was no different."

Brie chuckled sadly at herself. "Baron and the other

subs had to remind me that I had a significant victory because I can only see the battles left to fight."

"The process will take time, babygirl," he reminded her gently.

She sighed in frustration. "I wish I could go back to my old life and forget it ever happened."

"I know it's tempting, but psychological wounds don't magically go away. They must be acknowledged and dealt with before they worm their way into your psyche and wreak havoc in ways you cannot anticipate or control." He sighed. "Trust me, babygirl. I speak from experience."

She looked at Sir in admiration, appreciating how he'd taken his difficult past and worked hard to better himself—and help others because of it. In countless ways, she had benefitted from his determination to grow and learn from his past.

Wanting to reward him for his tenacious grit and determination, Brie said, "There's one more thing I learned today…" She paused for a moment, knowing the consequences of what she was about to say.

Grinning mischievously, she told him, "You are a very *wise* man, Sir."

Bedtime

Rytsar called regularly, but he still remained in Russia for unexplained reasons. Tonight, he'd requested a chance to sing to the children at bedtime, so Brie started with Antony. Laying him down in the crib, she tucked him in and then held the phone above her son's face so he could see Rytsar.

Antony smiled and reached up, wanting to touch his *dyadya.*

As soon as Rytsar began singing the hauntingly beautiful Russian lullaby, Brie saw Antony start to relax. She was not surprised when he fell fast asleep after only two renditions.

Tiptoeing out of the room, Brie shut off the light and quietly shut the door. "You truly have a magical voice," she whispered.

Rytsar smirked. "It pales in comparison to my magical tongue, *radost moya.*"

"I can attest to that," she agreed, blushing as she imagined that tongue pleasing her.

Brie entered Hope's room next and smiled at her little girl, who was already in bed hugging the white horse Rytsar had given her.

"I have a special surprise for you, sweet pea."

Kneeling beside the toddler's bed, Brie held out the phone. The moment Hope saw Rytsar, she cried joyously, "*Dyadya*!"

The grin on Rytsar's face melted Brie's heart.

"Is *moye solntse* ready to sleep?" he asked her.

Hope nodded while squeezing the neck of her horse tightly with both arms. Rytsar started slowly, lingering on each word as he sang to her.

Brie smiled to herself when she saw Hope's eyelids starting to droop.

By the time he finished the last line, "*…wish you sweet dreams while you sleep…*" Hope was already in dreamland.

Brie grinned as she turned off the light and shut the door. "That was truly beautiful, Rytsar."

"Not as beautiful as you."

Brie giggled as she headed downstairs, but her smile faltered after a moment. "I miss you."

"That was part of the reason I called tonight."

She instantly perked up. "What do you mean?"

"It wasn't just the children I wanted to put to bed tonight."

Brie grinned. "What do you have in mind?"

"Do you see your Master?" he asked with a sexy smirk.

Brie glanced in the kitchen, then looked over at Sir's office and noticed it was dark. Curious, she headed to the bedroom but found it empty also.

Giggling, she admitted, "I think I've lost him."

"Did you try out back?"

She immediately headed out to the backyard, and there she found Sir sitting in the hot tub with a martini waiting for her.

"Take off your clothes, *radost moya*, and join him," Rytsar commanded.

Slipping off her dress, Brie shimmied out of her underwear and quickly joined Sir in the hot tub. She purred as she slid into the warm, bubbling water.

When Sir pulled her to him, she noticed he was also naked. "Well, hello, Sir!"

He chuckled, kissing her deeply as his erect cock pressed against her thigh.

"I am sitting in my hot tub as well, *radost moya*, watching the morning sun light up the sky," Rytsar informed her.

Brie looked up at the crescent moon above her and joked, "Our lives are like night and day."

"*Da…*" he laughed. "Let us toast to sharing this unique moment."

Brie set the cell phone down on the edge of the hot tub, picked up her martini glass, and clinked it against Sir's, echoing, "To the moment."

As she sat there, enjoying the cool drink and the warm water, Brie asked Rytsar, "Are you naked, too?"

"But of course."

She giggled, imagining him lying naked in his hot tub, leisurely staring out at Moscow as he watched the people scurry below as the city came to life.

After several minutes of idle chat between the men,

Rytsar asked, "Radost moya, do you see the red box?"

Brie scanned their small backyard and spied it on a table set against the hot tub. "I do!"

Getting out of the water long enough to open the box and take out its contents, Brie returned to Sir's side and admired the phallus constructed to Rytsar's exact proportions.

"Do you consent to playing with me?" Rytsar asked huskily.

Brie was touched that her sexy sadist was honoring her current need for control. "I do, Rytsar."

"You will play with yourself using my cock while your Master teases you."

Sir momentarily lifted Brie out of the water and placed her on his lap facing away from him. She enjoyed the fact his hard shaft rested between her buttocks. He then spread her legs wide before cupping her breasts with both hands. Brie felt shivers as he kissed her neck, grazing his teeth over her throat.

She turned on the phallus and watched the purple lights race up the shaft. Slipping it between her legs, she began rubbing the head of it against her pussy.

Rytsar groaned loudly, letting her know that he was wearing his own device and could feel everything she was doing.

Brie exposed more of her throat to Sir when he began rolling her nipples between his fingers, tugging on them lightly as he nibbled her neck. In that moment, she felt luxuriously spoiled. She imagined Rytsar teasing her with his shaft while Sir's cock pressed against her ass, hinting at a session of double penetration.

Needing more stimulation, Brie slowly slipped the phallus inside her pussy and delighted in Rytsar's vocal appreciation. "It has been too long," he stated in a strained voice.

Squeezing one of her breasts, Sir slipped his other hand between her legs and teased her clit while she slowly thrust the dildo in and out of her pussy. She was enjoying herself a little too much, failing to realize she was giving Rytsar maximum stimulation.

It wasn't until he groaned in pleasurable agony, saying, "Your sub is being merciless, *moy droog*" that she realized what she has been doing.

Brie immediately stopped her thrusting, not wanting to push the sexy Russian over the edge just yet.

"I have a remedy for that," Sir replied smoothly.

He lifted Brie off his lap and ordered her to bend over the edge of the hot tub. She eagerly agreed and watched with excitement as he leaned over to grab a bottle of lubricant.

"Coat the phallus liberally," he commanded.

Brie bit her lip as Sir squirted a quarter-sized amount of the gel into her hand, then watched as she rubbed it over the sex toy. Rytsar's grunts of pleasure only turned her on even more.

Sir stood up in the hot tub, the water dripping from his body as he positioned himself behind her and slowly pushed his cock into her pussy. Once he was deep inside, he began slowly stroking her with his cock. The sound and feel of the water splashing around them with each thrust only added to the sensual experience.

Sir growled hungrily. "I am going to watch as you

penetrate your ass with the phallus, téa."

Brie felt sensual butterflies when she heard his command. "Yes, Master!"

Sir then thrust his cock in deeper and held still, watching her as she placed the tip of the phallus against her tight rosette. She pushed it into her ass centimeter by centimeter, the girth of the dildo stretching her open.

As her inner muscles tightened around his phallus, Brie was rewarded when she heard Rytsar's sharp intake of breath.

"*Blyad…*" Rytsar groaned.

Sir took hold of her wrist, helping her to force the phallus even deeper. Then he grabbed her hips with both hands and began thrusting again. Not wanting to disturb the neighbors, Brie held back her moans as she grabbed the edge of the hot tub and took Sir's hard strokes.

The beauty of Rytsar's instrument was that it was so sensitive, he could feel when her inner muscles began to tighten around the toy just before she orgasmed.

"She is ready to climax, *moy droog*," Rytsar growled hoarsely, "and I plan to join her."

Brie covered her mouth, her muffled cries of ecstasy joining Rytsar's as she came. She swore she could feel the toy throbbing inside her as he climaxed.

Erotic chills added to her excitement as they orgasmed together.

Sir slowed down to enjoy her climax, but as soon as it ended, he ramped right back up. Brie had to cover her mouth to keep from screaming in pleasure as the warm water splashed furiously around them.

The moment Sir released inside her, a second orgasm

took Brie by surprise. Both men groaned in unison as her inner muscles squeezed tight, pulsing in rhythmic bursts. Afterward, Brie was left panting heavily. She slowly pulled the toy from her, gently setting it down on the side of the hot tub.

"Thank you, Rytsar," she purred as she turned the toy off.

Sir finished the last of his martini before grabbing a towel and holding it open for her. She sighed in contentment as she stood up and he wrapped her in its fluffy goodness.

After toweling himself off and wrapping the towel around his waist, Sir picked her up and slung her over his shoulder like a caveman. He carried her into the house while she clutched the phone, giggling at Rytsar.

Once inside, he headed to the bedroom and set her down. Brie collapsed onto the bed in pleasurable exhaustion, telling Rytsar, "Just like the children, you have me ready to fall asleep."

He chuckled. "And you have given me the perfect *start* to my day."

Sir lay down beside her and asked him, "How are things going, old friend?"

"Better than expected."

Sir seemed to perk up at his answer. "I'm glad to hear that."

"Nothing is settled yet, but each day, I am getting closer."

Brie noticed the relief on Sir's face, which piqued her curiosity. But, before she could question him on it, Rytsar asked, "How is it going for you, *moy droog*?"

Sir glanced at Brie before speaking. "My father-in-law is a difficult man but, ironically, he and I are on the same page when it comes to Holloway." Clenching his fist, Sir growled, "Jail is not good enough for the monster."

"*Da*," Rytsar stated coldly. "I am looking into it."

Brie sat up in alarm, suddenly no longer tired.

"Neither of you can get involved! If something happens to Holloway in jail, you two could be questioned. And if you were to get caught…" Her voice broke. It terrified her just to think about it.

"I can't let him steal anything else from me!"

The next day, she was faced with the very same discussion. This time, it involved her father. Sir went to answer the door and looked startled when he checked to see who it was before opening the door.

"Your parents are here."

Brie was surprised. Her father hadn't spoken to Sir since he last visited their home.

Sir was quick to usher them inside amid the shouts from the few remaining reporters clamoring for attention. "This is an unexpected visit."

Her father stated curtly, "I felt it was necessary, Thane."

Brie stood in the hallway, holding Antony. She met her father's gaze, keeping her voice calm. "Daddy, do you have anything to say?"

She fully expected him to apologize to Sir.

Glancing down at the floor, her father answered in a low and enraged voice, "I need that bastard to die!"

Brie was shocked. "No, Daddy! Holloway will be punished to the full extent of the law and will remain in prison until his last breath."

Her father shook his head. "I don't trust the law, little girl. Especially with the influence that man has. He is a rabid animal that needs to be put down. Prison is too good for that bastard!"

Sir stayed silent, although Brie knew he agreed with her father.

"Daddy," Brie stated firmly, determined to change the subject. "Don't you have something to say to my husband?"

Brie leaned her head against Sir's shoulder for emphasis.

Her father glanced at Sir uncomfortably. Instead of apologizing, he just broke down.

"I love you, Brianna, and I hate what's happened to you. Holloway needs to be put down now! I can't think about anything else."

Her mother stood beside him, looking helplessly at Brie with tears in her eyes. Brie remembered that same look from years past. It meant, *You know how your father can get…*

Taking a deep breath, Brie said more firmly, "The last time you were here, you said that you wished Thane had never come into my life. But you don't understand, Daddy. He has been the rock I've depended on through all of this. You have no idea what a good man he is." She shook her head in disbelief. "He even defends you when you've been nothing but disrespectful and rude to him."

Sir touched Brie's arm, stating quietly, "Everyone has been affected by what's happened, babygirl."

Brie's father looked stricken but remained silent, refusing to apologize.

Sir turned to her parents, stating solemnly, "Right now, Brie needs to concentrate on healing from the psychological damage she's experienced. It is imperative that we *all* support her in that."

Her father huffed. "I have no problem supporting my daughter, Thane. But the man who kidnapped her has a team of lawyers and is hellbent on getting out of jail. If that happens, think of the message it will send to all of the other freaks like him. Have you considered that?"

Brie's mother broke her silence. Leaving her husband's side, she took Brie's hands in hers, saying earnestly, "I'll do anything to help you, sweetheart. Just name it."

Brie's eyes filled with unshed tears. "All I need is your continued support and unconditional love, Mama." She then looked at her father. "Same goes for you, Daddy."

He blinked slowly several times, clearly unaffected by her plea.

Brie's mother gave her father a frightened look. "Bill, let's not repeat the past."

"Marcy, drop it!" he barked, his eyes suddenly trained on her. "You promised you wouldn't say anything."

Brie wondered what her father meant. What secret was he keeping from her?

"So…" her mother said in a soft but commanding voice, "…you and I agree we will concentrate *only* on our daughter?"

Her father slowly nodded his head.

Brie's mother turned to Sir and smiled tenderly. "Thane, we are grateful for all the love and support you have shown our daughter. I know this has been hard on you as well."

Sir nodded. "It has."

Even though Brie knew the relationship between her father and husband remained strained, her father thrust out his hand to Sir. "I'm willing to take it one day at a time, son."

It was not an apology, but Sir accepted the truce and shook her father's hand firmly.

While her parents were leaving, however, Brie noticed her dad turned to Sir. She distinctly heard him say under his breath, "If you don't take care of the problem, I will."

Brie didn't miss the grave look in Sir's eyes as he shut the front door.

Will You

Amidst the uncertainties in Brie's life, something truly beautiful was happening.

Master Anderson arrived at their house, wanting to check in before the big event. "Are you sure you've got everything?"

Sir opened the camera bag. "Yes, but you can check for yourself if you want to."

Master Anderson waved his hand as if he trusted his friend but then checked the bag anyway. "Just want to be sure… I mean, it's not like I can have a 'do over' if I mess anything up."

Sir chuckled. "You have nothing to worry about. The only thing that matters is her saying yes, and that's guaranteed."

Master Anderson shook his head. "You don't understand, buddy. I want this to be *perfect* down to the very last detail."

Brie grinned. "Master Anderson, I'm sure it will be lovely and everything Shey could ever dream of, but Sir is right. The only thing she is going to remember is that moment you get down on your knee and slip the ring on her finger."

She was charmed by the pink blush rising in Master Anderson's cheeks.

"I've never met anyone like her, and I want this proposal to be as classy and beautiful as she is. Have I showed you the ring yet?"

Brie's eyes widened. "No, but I would love to see it!"

Master Anderson started patting his pockets frantically. "I swear I brought it…" His face suddenly lit up, "There it is…" Pulling a small blue ring box from his pocket, he grinned at Brie as he opened it.

"Oh, Master Anderson!" she squealed as she looked at the ring. It was a beautiful French cut diamond with a row of smaller diamonds set in the band. "It's absolutely exquisite."

"Just like Shey," he agreed. "It took me months to find the right one."

"That's a lot of searching."

He nodded. "It was long and hard."

"That's what she said," Brie retorted.

Master Anderson suddenly burst out laughing and slapped Brie hard on the back—so hard, she almost lost her balance.

He immediately grabbed Brie's shoulders to hold her steady and apologized, "I didn't mean to send you flying, young Brie. I'm just a little excitable right now."

Brie giggled. "That's all right. I kind of like seeing you like this. All nervous and jittery. It's cute."

He gave her a half-grin. "Glad I could entertain you."

"So, are you satisfied with the camera equipment?" Sir asked with a smirk.

"Wait! Let me finish looking through it."

Smiling at Brie, Sir shook his head while Master Anderson meticulously checked each item in the bag.

"Looks good," he finally announced. "So, the plan is you head off to the restaurant at six. The staff will show you exactly where to sit. You guys will have plenty of time to set up while I change clothes before picking up Shey and her parents. My family will join you there. So, if any issues arise, they can help."

"Aww…you had your family fly out, too?" Brie asked him.

"Of course!" Master Anderson replied, laughing. "You have no idea how long my family has been waiting for this moment." He glanced at Sir. "Remember how determined I was to find the right 'shoe' in college?"

Sir stroked his chin thoughtfully. "I do. I also remember the empty plate of brownies, and my new roommate telling me he had eight sisters who'd eaten them all."

Master Anderson ran his hand through his hair, laughing. "Man, you were so gullible back then."

Sir gave him a droll look. "How was I to know you were a liar?"

"Not a liar," Master Anderson corrected. "I prefer the term 'creative fabricator'. It was all in good fun." He smacked Sir on the back. "And we sure did have a lot of fun back then, didn't we, buddy?"

Sir put his arm around Brie. "I'd say you and I have far more fun now."

"You got that right." Master Anderson rubbed his hands together excitedly. "Not only have I found the perfect shoe, but she's damn beautiful inside and out."

"She is," Brie agreed.

Master Anderson suddenly scanned the area, asking, "Is there anything I've forgotten?"

Sir placed his hand on Master Anderson's shoulder. "The night will go flawlessly. There's nothing to worry about."

"You're right, buddy," he said, nodding. "Everything is in place." He winked at Brie. "The only thing left is for my future fiancée to say yes."

Sir chuckled after shutting the door behind Master Anderson. "I've never seen the man so rattled."

Brie giggled. "It's the sweetest thing ever."

While Brie was grabbing her purse before heading out with Sir, a flash of blue caught her eye. "Oh, no!"

"What's wrong?" Sir asked, hoisting the camera bag onto his shoulder.

Brie bent down to pick up the velvet ring box. "Master Anderson must have dropped this when he slapped me on the back so enthusiastically."

Sir laughed when he saw the box. "Anderson has certainly enjoyed pranking me over the years. I think it's time I repay the favor."

Brie's eye widened. "What are you planning to do, Sir?"

"Nothing…for now," he said with a sly grin, taking the box from her and slipping it into his pocket "I can't imagine how bad he's going to sweat once he figures out he lost it. Won't that make for a fun conversation in the years to come?"

Brie stared at him dumbfounded. "You never cease to surprise me, Sir."

He tweaked her nose. "That's how I prefer it."

The drive was beautiful. Brie couldn't help but admire the scenery flashing by once they got to the winding roads leading up to the hilltop restaurant. She could understand why Master Anderson had chosen this place. The view of LA was breathtaking and made the perfect backdrop for his proposal.

The owner greeted them personally. She was thrilled to help execute Master Anderson's proposal. "I enjoy getting to play cupid in situations like this," she confessed to Brie as she led them to their table.

While Sir was setting up the camera equipment, the owner pointed to a large empty table on the opposite side of the ornate half-wall that separated them. "Shey will be sitting here, so you'll be out of her line of sight, but you can still get the quality shots you're looking for."

"Babygirl, can you sit there so I can take a few practice shots?" Sir asked her.

Sitting down in Shey's assigned chair, Brie pretended that Master Anderson was proposing to her and made sure to wear a properly shocked expression.

"Is everything okay, miss?"

Brie blushed and turned in her chair, coming face to face with a large "package" outlined in a tight-fitting pair of jeans. She looked up to see a handsome older gentleman grinning down at her.

Brie popped out of the chair and held out her hand to Master Anderson's dad. "It's lovely to see you again, Mr. Anderson."

While she was shaking hands with the man, she glanced over at his wife and their three daughters. "You all must be so excited!"

Instead of answering, Brie was tackled by Master Anderson's three sisters hugging her all at once. She glanced over to see Sir lowering his camera and smiling at her.

"When Brad first told us about Shey, we knew she was the one," Master Anderson's mother told Brie, her green eyes sparkling with delight.

"Is there anything we can do to help?" his father asked.

Sir walked up to them and set the camera down. He was given the same enthusiastic hugs from Master Anderson's sisters. It warmed Brie's heart to see the joy on Sir's face as he greeted Master Anderson's family.

She silently picked up the camera without anyone noticing and took a few shots to capture the moment.

Brie was surprised when Sir told the family about Master Anderson leaving the ring behind at their house. When they asked what Sir planned to do about it, the entire family broke out in laughter loving his idea.

Brie shook her head, thinking, *They're all crazy.*

When the owner returned to the table to tell them the valet was parking Master Anderson's truck, everyone quickly took their seats.

Brie's smile was so wide her lips almost hurt when she saw Master Anderson walking up to the table escorting Shey. He was dressed in a striking three-piece business suit and was wearing polished cowboy boots and his black Stetson.

Totally melt-worthy…

Shey wore a white gown decorated with silver filigree that beautifully highlighted her long curly red hair. Brie knew Master Anderson had picked out the dress first, and then planned his suit accordingly, wanting to complement Shey's dress. He'd explained to Brie earlier, "She is the star and I want her to shine tonight, like the diamond she is."

Brie had never seen Shey's parents before. They were an older couple and seemed especially shy and quiet as they sat down. It was an interesting contrast to Master Anderson's family, who were anything but shy.

Sir had the camera aimed at the group and was furiously taking pictures as the two families greeted each other.

Brie was lucky. They were seated close enough that she could hear their conversation and was soon treated to stories about both Master Anderson and Shey when they were young.

Christina, Master Anderson's youngest sister, piped up. "How did you two meet? I bet it was romantic…"

Master Anderson pushed his hat back, grinning at Shey. "If I recall right, I had a meeting with Carl, but you showed up instead."

Shey giggled. "I did."

Master Anderson leaned in close to Christina. "I bet

you didn't know this, but Shey is a real card shark. She beat the pants off me."

Shey's laughter went up an octave.

Brie had to stifle her own laughter, having heard all about their little game of strip poker the night they first met.

When the waiter came and passed out the menu, Brie heard Shey's father tsk when he saw the prices. "I know you said you were paying for the meal, but I insist on chipping in."

Master Anderson's father agreed. "Pay for yourself and your lovely date. I'll pick up my brood's share."

Master Anderson laughed at them both. "Absolutely not. I'm buying, and I won't take no for an answer." The two fathers opened up the menus again without complaint.

When the waiter came back over, everyone at the table, including Shey, ordered the cheapest meal on the menu.

Master Anderson told the waiter, "Let me have that ticket order."

When the man handed it to him, Master Anderson tore it into little pieces in front of everyone and asked the waiter, "Can you please give us a few minutes?"

Brie found it both sweet and hilarious. None of them knew that Master Anderson not only could afford the lavish dinner but could buy the entire restaurant if he wanted.

Looking at both families, Master Anderson told them, "I know you mean well, but please order whatever you want on the menu. Heck, you can even order two main courses if you like. I picked this restaurant because of the food, and I want you all to enjoy it." Putting his hand on his heart, he told them, "I will be severely insulted if you don't."

When the waiter returned, everyone seemed to take his words to heart. After writing it all down, the waiter nodded to Master Anderson. "I will send the first course out shortly."

It seemed the big moment was about to happen. Brie's heart started to race when Master Anderson started patting his pockets, looking for the ring.

"Time to see him sweat a little…" Sir chuckled to himself. He took several pictures of Master Anderson's growing anxiety as he checked every one of his pockets.

Shey couldn't help noticing he was agitated and asked, "What's wrong, Brad?"

"Nothing, honey," he replied, taking off his hat to swipe his brow.

Attempting to be nonchalant, he purposely dropped his napkin to take a quick peek under the table. When he came up empty, he glanced in Sir's direction, looking bereft.

Sir's face was perfectly stoic as he held back his laughter.

The waiter returned to the table with a young woman beside him. The girl was holding a handful of fresh-cut roses. "To celebrate the beauty represented at this table, we would like to present a rose to each of you fine ladies tonight."

While the young woman passed out the flowers, Brie noticed the waiter tapping on Master Anderson's shoulder and then discreetly handing him the blue box. The relief on Master Anderson's face was priceless.

"That was brilliant, Sir," Brie whispered.

He took his eye off the camera for a second and winked at her.

Brie felt giddy when she turned and saw Master Anderson standing up to address the table.

"As you all know, I think the world of the woman sitting beside me. Family means everything to both of us, which is one of the reasons I wanted us to gather tonight."

Shey looked up at Master Anderson lovingly.

"But that's not the only reason…"

Brie could hear Shey's audible gasp when Master Anderson slowly got down on one knee.

He opened the small box in his hand and held it out to her. "Shey Allen, will you do me the honor of being my wife?"

Shey put her hands to her mouth as she stared at the diamond ring. "Brad…"

Master Anderson didn't take his eyes off her while he patiently waited for her answer.

Looking at him with loving devotion, she said, "Yes, I will. I would love to be your wife!"

The entire restaurant broke out in applause as Master Anderson took Shey's hand and slipped the ring on her finger. Afterward, he picked her up and kissed her full on the mouth as he twirled her around.

Tears of joy filled Brie's eyes. In a world full of pain and misery, love had the power to unite souls together and make it a better place.

Brie couldn't stop smiling during the drive home. As they were walking in the door, she said, "That has got to be the sweetest proposal I have ever seen."

"They are certainly good together," Sir agreed, staring at his camera as he went through the hundreds of shots he'd taken during the evening.

Brie playfully slapped Sir on the butt. "Even with your little stunt."

Sir chuckled. "I think it added to the scene."

"I'm sure Brad's family would agree, but I really felt sorry for him when he realized he didn't have the ring with him."

Sir put the camera down and pulled her to him, squeezing her tight. "In the end, all the bells and whistles don't count for much. Anderson could have proposed in the middle of a grocery store with a rubber band for an engagement ring, and I guarantee she still would have said yes."

Brie hugged Sir, sighing with contentment. "You're right. When it's true love, nothing else matters."

Her phone suddenly rang, interrupting the pleasant moment. When Brie saw it was Mary, she immediately answered. "What's up?"

"Turn on the TV. Stat!"

When Sir saw Brie hastily picking up the remote, he asked, "What's going on?"

"I have no idea. Mary just said I needed to turn on the TV."

The moment she hit the power button, Brie saw a banner flashing across the screen reading "Breaking News".

She immediately recognized the prison where Holloway was being held. A reporter was standing outside the tall fence topped with barbed wire, as he spoke to the camera. "...we aren't being given details about the nature of his death. However, we can confirm that Greg Holloway was pronounced dead earlier this evening. Naturally, we will keep you informed as we get more information. If you are not familiar with the case, Greg Holloway was arrested after—"

Sir shut off the television and took the phone from Brie. Before hanging up, he told Mary, "Miss Wilson, thank you for apprising us of the situation. I sincerely hope this news provides you with a sense of closure."

Brie stared at him in utter shock, her heart threatening to beat out of her chest wondering if he was somehow involved with Holloway's death.

"Sir?" she whimpered, her voice trembling with fear.

Shockwaves

"Did…" She pointed at the blank television screen with a shaking finger. "…you…?"

Brie couldn't even say it out loud.

"Did I what? Wish him dead? Absolutely."

"But did you…?"

"Have the bastard killed? No, I wanted to do it with my bare hands. I needed to look him in the eyes when I ended his life," Sir replied in a voice so dark it chilled Brie to the bone.

Picking up his phone, Sir immediately called Rytsar and put him on speaker. "Are you alone?" he asked.

"*Nyet.* Should I be?" he replied, laughing. "Up for another kinky session so soon, *moy droog*?"

"We need to talk."

Recognizing the gravity of the situation based on Sir's tone, Rytsar told him, "Give me a moment."

After several minutes, he addressed them again, "I am alone now. Feel free to speak."

Before Sir could open his mouth, Brie cried, "How

could you!"

Rytsar grunted. "I had to do what was best for you, *radost moya*. Surely you understand that?"

Sir immediately jumped in. "Brianna is asking about the death of Greg Holloway."

"*What?*" Rytsar suddenly roared.

"Greg Holloway died earlier this evening and we…" Sir looked at Brie, "would both like to hear what you know about it."

"*Blyad!*" Rytsar howled.

"I need to know what happened," Sir pressed.

"How would I know, *moy droog*? My men have been busy working out the details. I failed to take into account what a complicated mess your penal system is."

"Wait…" Brie muttered, relief suddenly flowing through her. "You're saying you didn't have anything to do with Holloway's death tonight?"

Rytsar spat angrily. "Unfortunately, it seems someone got to him first. I had the perfect scenario planned for the maggot." He let out an ominous growl. "He would have suffered greatly for what he has done. How did he die?"

"That's why we called you," Sir answered. "The authorities haven't released any details about the cause of his death."

"Whatever he died of was not nearly painful enough!" Rytsar snarled.

Brie exclaimed, "I'm just relieved you weren't involved, Rytsar!"

"But, the question remains unanswered," Sir stated.

She felt her stomach twist into a painful knot. If neither Sir nor Rytsar did it, then that left only one other person.

Oh, my God, Daddy. What did you do?

Brie was unsure if she wanted to know…

Brie woke up to the doorbell ringing relentlessly.

Sir pulled the covers back and jumped out of bed, slipping on a pair of sweats before heading to the door. "Whoever it is, I'm about to give them hell!"

After throwing on her robe and cinching it tight, Brie hurried to join him.

Sir took a quick peek before frowning. "It's your father."

Brie suddenly felt sick.

Growing impatient, her father resorted to pounding on the door. Sir immediately opened it and pulled him inside.

The man was holding a paper bag and had a silly grin on his face.

"Where's Mom?" Brie asked in concern.

"She didn't want to come," he muttered. "But, no matter…"

Brie felt unsteady and grabbed on to the chair near her.

Her father then turned to stare at Thane, beaming. "I have never been prouder, son!"

Sir furrowed his brow. "Why?"

"Don't play coy with me. I've come here to celebrate!" He pulled away the brown paper bag to reveal a bottle of champagne. Twisting off the wire cap, he jimmied the cork until it made a resounding pop.

Her father looked at Brie guiltily. "Sorry. I didn't think about waking the children."

Brie stood staring at him with her jaw hanging open, feeling sicker by the moment. "Daddy, what have you done?"

He snorted. "I told you. I've come to celebrate!"

He gave Sir a resounding slap on the back. "Now, I'm not much of a drinking man, but here we are. Where are your glasses?"

Sir took the bottle of champagne from him and set it on the counter. "You need to explain yourself."

Her father looked from Sir to Brie, then back to Sir. He straightened his back and cleared his throat. "Look, I get it. I'm familiar with this kind of situation. But let me give you some sage advice, son. They find out. They always find out. Best to be open with Brianna now."

"I have no idea what you are talking about," Sir replied sternly.

Her father chuckled. "You have a great poker face, Thane. I'll grant you that. However, it serves no purpose now." He pointed at Brie. "You can tell she's already questioning you."

"The only thing I'm questioning is *you*, Daddy," Brie stated.

Her father shook his head. "Whatever you say stays with me. I swear it. I won't even tell your mother, although she already suspects."

"Suspects what?" Brie demanded.

"That Thane took care of the problem."

Brie was left momentarily stunned and stammered, "I was afraid you…did it." She refused to voice what "it" was.

Her father shook his head and looked at Sir as if he were disappointed. "What? You weren't involved?"

"No. However, I was considering my options."

Nodding in understanding, her father glanced at the champagne and shrugged. "Well, we have even more reason to celebrate then. We don't have to worry about it anymore, the bastard's dead."

For the very first time, Brie let Holloway's death sink in.

He can never hurt me or Mary again…

A world without Holloway in it was ripe with possibilities. Still…

"I need a moment," she murmured, heading back to the bedroom.

As she lay down on the bed, the conversation she and Sir had with Rytsar started replaying in her mind.

"I had to do what was best for you, radost moya. Surely you understand that…"

Brie picked up her phone to call him.

"You are up early, *radost moya!*" Rytsar answered, sounding pleased.

"I need something from you."

"What?" he asked good-naturedly. "Just say the word and it's yours."

She clutched the phone, preparing for the worst when she asked, "I need to know what you are keeping from me. I'm tired of being kept in the dark."

"Have you spoken to your Master about it?"

"No, Rytsar. I'm asking you to tell me—right here, right now."

He let out a long, painful sigh.

She tried to reason with him. "Do you remember how it felt when you knew the Koslov brothers were dead and you were finally free?"

"*Da*," he answered somberly.

"That's how I am feeling right now. Holloway can't hurt me anymore, so you don't need to protect me from whatever you are hiding."

"I hear you, *radost moya*," he replied, groaning to himself.

Brie was nervous, waiting for him to speak. She knew she'd won the argument, but she was unsure if she could handle what he was about to say.

"I would rather spare you the truth."

"I *need* to hear it," she insisted.

"Very well." Rytsar sighed and then paused a long moment.

Brie held her breath, needing to hear the secret he'd kept for so long…

"The creature escaped from the convent, *radost moya*. The Reverend Mother was attacked and was badly injured."

The blood drained from Brie's face. "No…"

She closed her eyes and groaned in misery, understanding why he had chosen to stay silent.

Rytsar was quick to assure her, "The creature has no passport and is effectively trapped in Russia. Even as we speak, my men are closing in on her. It won't be long before she is captured and safely locked up."

"That's why you couldn't come..." Brie muttered as all the small pieces started coming together.

"*Da.* Your well-being is the only thing that matters, which is why your Master and I agreed to stay silent."

"I feel numb..." she murmured faintly.

"You have suffered much, but you are strong, *radost moya.*"

All the anger she'd felt toward Rytsar about keeping his "secret" suddenly evaporated as reality set in. Even though Rytsar had rescued Tatianna from the slave traders, Brie knew he'd lost her months later when she committed suicide. Tatianna had been unable to handle the damage done to her soul.

After being rescued from a similar situation, Brie could only imagine how fearful Rytsar must have been that the same might happen to her—especially if she were to find out that Lilly had escaped.

"I will be okay, Rytsar," Brie assured him. "But...I am worried about you."

"Don't be," he insisted. "The creature may be ruthless, but I am a Durov and my wrath runs deep."

After her call to Rytsar, Brie stumbled out of the bedroom.

Sir frowned the moment he saw her. "Are you okay, Brie?"

The second she met Sir's gaze, she could tell he knew

what had transpired in the bedroom.

Oblivious, her father tried to hand her a glass of champagne to toast Holloway's demise.

Sir took it from him. "Brie needs time."

Without any further explanation, Sir escorted her father out of the house. When he returned, Sir held out his arms to her.

Brie gratefully walked into his embrace and started to cry. "Poor Reverend Mother…"

She could hear the pain in his voice when he answered, "Yes."

Sir held her tight as Brie slowly came to grips with the fact that Lilly remained a real and present threat.

New Heights

The next morning, Sir woke Brie up well before sunrise. While she was still groggy from sleep, he tossed her a set of clothes and said, "Get dressed, babygirl."

Donning them quickly, Brie headed out of the bedroom to find Sir bundling up Hope and Antony as he got ready to leave the house.

"Where are we going, Sir?"

"I think it is high time we redeem one of our wedding gifts," he answered.

Without further explanation, Sir dropped the children off at Unc's house. Judy met them at the door still dressed in her nightgown. "Are you hungry, Hope? I made a giant stack of pancakes for you and Jonathan."

Hope instantly perked up. "Jon-Jon?"

"Yep, cutie. He's in the kitchen with Unckie Jack."

The moment Brie set her daughter down, Hope started toddling down the hallway to the kitchen.

Judy took Antony from Sir, grinning. "You two go

off and have fun!"

"We plan to, Auntie," Sir replied, giving her a peck on the cheek. "Thanks again for agreeing to watch the kids on such short notice."

"You know we're happy to, even at this early hour," she assured him. Laughing, she added, "We told Jonathan that Hope was coming to visit last night, and he decided to wake up *extra* early this morning."

Brie grinned. "I love that they get along so well."

"The two are inseparable. It's the cutest dang thing."

Back in the car, Sir continued driving north to Santa Barbara. As soon as Brie saw the empty field with a hot air balloon, she squeaked in excitement. "I've always wanted to ride in one of those!"

"This gift is compliments of Captain. I had to check to see if the company would still honor the certificate since it is years old now. Thankfully, they were extremely gracious about it."

Brie stared at the brightly colored balloon, loving how the rainbow hues contrasted beautifully with the early morning sky.

The pilot and his crew walked up to greet them. "It's an honor to have you ride with us today, Mr. and Mrs. Davis."

"The honor is all ours." Brie grinned as she stared up at the giant balloon.

After giving them a short safety briefing, the pilot announced they were ready to take off. Sir helped support Brie as she slid one foot into the foothold on the side of the basket and threw her other leg over to jump in.

Once Sir joined her, Brie grabbed his hand, squeezing it excitedly while she watched the pilot activate the large burner.

Hot air swirled around them as the pilot began releasing the sandbags one by one. Brie could feel the basket start to move beneath her, and she imagined that the hot air balloon was as impatient as she was to take off.

Holding her breath, Brie braced herself. Finally, the balloon lifted off the ground. But it was gentle, not jolting like she was expecting.

Leaving the confines of the Earth almost had a dream-like quality to it as they slowly began to float upward. Brie looked down, marveling at everything as the ground became increasingly smaller.

It was surprisingly quiet—so quiet, in fact, she could hear the tiny cattle mooing as the balloon slowly drifted over a pasture.

Sir nudged Brie, pointing to the left. She couldn't believe it when two large California condors soared past them. They flew so close to the balloon that she felt as if she could reach out and touch the one closest to her.

Turning to Sir, she whispered, "This is pure magic!"

He nodded, clearly as awestruck by seeing the pair of condors as she was.

After the condors flew off, the pilot turned on the burners and headed even higher. Once the balloon leveled off, he informed them that they were now three thousand feet in the air.

Brie looked down at the world below her, marveling at the beauty of the Santa Ynez Mountains as they were silently carried along by the breeze.

In a state of awe, she told Sir, "The world looks so different from up here. There are so many things you miss because you can't take in everything when you are down in it."

He wrapped his arms around her. "Isn't it amazing how a fresh perspective can completely change your view of things?"

Brie smiled, leaning into him. "I've never felt such peace before."

She turned her head to the pilot and smiled. "I wish I could stay up here forever."

He smiled awkwardly. "I'm sure that can be arranged."

Brie laughed. "Wouldn't that be lovely?"

As they gently floated above the hills and valleys, Brie was struck again by how quiet it was. She closed her eyes for a moment to soak up the profound tranquility she felt.

When she opened them again, she noticed the pilot looking at her strangely, while a bead of sweat slowly rolled down his forehead.

The hairs rose on the back of her neck, and she gripped Sir as she watched the man reach into his front jacket pocket. Brie's life suddenly flashed before her eyes as he pulled out something long and black.

Her voice caught when she tried to cry out a warning. "He's…got a—"

Then she saw it.

The pilot's awkward smile returned when he held it out to her. "I made this…for you, Mrs. Davis."

Still mute with shock, Brie stared down at a pretty leather paddle of black and red with heart cut-outs decorating it.

"My wife and I were inspired to dip our toes into BDSM after watching your documentary, and we've never looked back. I now run a leather shop specializing in BDSM tools, and I wanted you to have this, Mrs. Davis."

Brie held out her hands, commanding them not to shake as she took the tool from him. She was too embarrassed to look the man in the eye when she said breathlessly, "It's beautiful."

She glanced at Sir and squeaked, "Won't this be fun?"

Covering for her nervousness, Sir took the instrument from Brie to study it. Slapping the paddle against his hand, he nodded appreciatively. "This is of exceptional quality. I look forward to utilizing it during our next session."

The pilot's face lit up. "I…I'm flattered that you would consider using it."

When Sir put his arm around Brie to support her, she was certain he could feel her trembling.

"I would never let a fine quality tool go to waste, especially when it was hand-crafted by an artisan with such skill," he complimented the pilot.

The man looked at Brie and asked anxiously, "Would you mind if I took a picture with you for my wife?"

Her fear fading, Brie smiled and turned to Sir. "Would that be fine with you, Sir?"

"Only if you are comfortable with the request," he

answered.

"I am."

Sir took the man's phone to take the pictures while Brie moved over to the pilot. Her smile was genuine when she looked into the camera.

Brie realized what Sir said about having a fresh perspective applied to her own life as well. After suffering intense torture at Holloway's hands, simple interactions had now taken on a sinister tone for her.

It seemed all her experiences were filtered through that lens now.

But that was not how she wanted to live.

Although she understood why she'd lost her perspective, flying above the Earth had reminded her just how beautiful life was.

Brie had the man of her dreams standing next to her, and two children she loved more than life itself. She also had a group of friends who had proven their loyalty and love for her countless times. And, if that weren't enough, across the ocean, she had a sexy Russian making sure she was being kept safe.

Brie wanted to pursue her life without fear so she could fully embrace the future ahead. She didn't want to hide from it.

Anything less would not be true to who she was as a person and a submissive.

Brie smiled and nodded to the pilot, grateful for the lesson he'd unknowingly taught her.

On the drive home Brie remained silent, reliving the incredible balloon ride.

"How are you faring, babygirl?"

She laughed self-consciously. "Well, other than thinking the poor man had a gun and was going to kill me, I'm doing great."

Brie then looked at Sir in concern. "Do you think he knew?"

Sir chuckled. "No. He was so nervous about giving you his gift that he seemed oblivious to everything else."

"Thank goodness! He was nothing but kind to us."

"It's evident you had a big impact on his life."

Brie reached over to pat his arm. "It was a team effort, Sir. Without you, I would never have realized the joys of BDSM."

He smiled, keeping his eyes on the road.

Brie heard his phone notify him that he had a text. Sir pulled it out from his pocket and asked, "Do you mind checking it?"

"My pleasure, Sir." Clicking his messages, Brie noticed he had a new message from Marquis Gray. Her jaw dropped when she read the text.

Sir glanced at her. "Anything wrong?"

Brie stared at him, unable to hide her shock. "It's from Marquis Gray."

Frowning, Sir asked, "What does it say, babygirl?"

Brie read his text out loud, her stomach twisting in fear for Marquis.

I believe I may be responsible for Greg Holloway's death.

I hope you enjoyed ***Whispered Promises!***

Reviews mean the world to me.

TWO BOOKS COMING UP NEXT

Beneath the Flames & Sir's Destiny!

Beneath the Flames:

Brie's Submission Book 25

(Dec 8, 2022)

The next book in the Brie Series will take your breath away.

Get ready for some wicked fun

~~~~~~

(Sept 1, 2022)

Sir's Destiny

Standalone in the Unleashed Series

Join Thane Davis in his journey to become Headmaster of the Submissive Training Center!

"Destiny is calling…"
~~~~~~

COMING NEXT

Beneath the Flames

Brie's Submission
Book 25

Available for Preorder

Sir's Destiny

Unleashed Series
Book 3

Available for Preorder

Reviews mean the world to me!

I truly appreciate you taking the time to review ***Whispered Promises***.

If you could leave a review on both Goodreads and the site where you purchased this book from, I would be so grateful. Sincerely, ~Red

ABOUT THE AUTHOR

Over Two Million readers have enjoyed Red's stories

Red Phoenix – USA Today Bestselling Author
Winner of 8 Readers' Choice Awards

Hey Everyone!

I'm Red Phoenix, an author who also happens to be a submissive in real life. I wrote the Brie's Submission series because I wanted people everywhere to know just how much fun BDSM can be.

There is a huge cast of characters who are part of Brie's journey. The further you read into the story the more you learn about each one. I hope you grow to love Brie and the gang as much as I do.

They've become like family.

When I'm not writing, you can find me online with readers.

I heart my fans! ~Red

To find out more visit my Website

redphoenixauthor.com

Follow Me on BookBub

bookbub.com/authors/red-phoenix

Newsletter: Sign up

redphoenixauthor.com/newsletter-signup

Facebook: AuthorRedPhoenix

Twitter: @redphoenix69

Instagram: RedPhoenixAuthor

I invite you to join my reader Group!

facebook.com/groups/539875076052037

SIGN UP FOR MY NEWSLETTER HERE FOR THE LATEST RED PHOENIX UPDATES

FOLLOW ME ON INSTAGRAM

INSTAGRAM.COM/REDPHOENIXAUTHOR

SALES, GIVEAWAYS, NEW RELEASES, PREORDER LINKS, AND MORE!

SIGN UP HERE

REDPHOENIXAUTHOR.COM/NEWSLETTER-SIGNUP

Red Phoenix is the author of:

Brie's Submission Series:

Teach Me #1
Love Me #2
Catch Me #3
Try Me #4
Protect Me #5
Hold Me #6
Surprise Me #7
Trust Me #8
Claim Me #9
Enchant Me #10
A Cowboy's Heart #11
Breathe with Me #12
Her Russian Knight #13
Under His Protection #14
Her Russian Returns #15
In Sir's Arms #16
Bound by Love #17
Tied to Hope #18
Hope's First Christmas #19
Secrets of the Heart #20
Her Sweet Surrender #21
The Ties That Bind #22
A Heart Unchained #23
Whispered Promises #24

***You can also purchase the** AUDIO BOOK **Versions**

Also part of the Submissive Training Center world:

Rise of the Dominates Trilogy
Sir's Rise
Master's Fate
The Russian Reborn

Captain's Duet
Safe Haven #1
Destined to Dominate #2

Unleashed Series
The Russian Unleashed #1
The Cowboy's Secret #2

Other Books by Red Phoenix

Blissfully Undone
* Available in eBook and paperback

(Snowy Fun—Two people find themselves snowbound in a cabin where hidden love can flourish, taking one couple on a sensual journey into ménage à trois)

His Scottish Pet: Dom of the Ages
* Available in eBook and paperback

Audio Book: *His Scottish Pet: Dom of the Ages*

(Scottish Dom—A sexy Dom escapes to Scotland in the late 1400s. He encounters a waif who has the potential to free him from his tragic curse)

The Only One

* Available in eBook and paperback

(Sexual Adventures—Fate has other plans but he's not letting her go…she is the only one!)

Passion is for Lovers

* Available in eBook and paperback

(Super sexy novelettes—*In 9 Days, 9 Days and Counting, And Then He Saved Me*, and *Play With Me at Noon*)

Varick: The Reckoning

* Available in eBook and paperback

(Savory Vampire—A dark, sexy vampire story. The hero navigates the dangerous world he has been thrust into with lusty passion and a pure heart)

eBooks

Keeper of the Wolf Clan (Keeper of Wolves, #1)

(Sexual Secrets—A virginal werewolf must act as the clan's mysterious Keeper)

The Keeper Finds Her Mate (Keeper of Wolves, #2)

(Second Chances—A young she-wolf must choose between old ties or new beginnings)

The Keeper Unites the Alphas (Keeper of Wolves, #3)

(Serious Consequences—The young she-wolf is captured by the rival clan)

Boxed Set: Keeper of Wolves Series (Books 1-3)

(Surprising Secrets—A secret so shocking it will rock Layla's world. The young she-wolf is put in a position of being able to save her werewolf clan or becoming the reason for its destruction)

Socrates Inspires Cherry to Blossom

(Satisfying Surrender—A mature and curvaceous woman becomes fascinated by an online Dom who has much to teach her)

By the Light of the Scottish Moon

(Saving Love—Two lost souls, the Moon, a werewolf, and a death wish…)

Play With Me at Noon

(Seeking Fulfillment—A desperate wife lives out her fantasies by taking five different men in five days)

Connect with Red on Substance B

Substance B is a platform for independent authors to directly connect with their readers. Please visit Red's Substance B page where you can:

- Sign up for Red's newsletter
- Send a message to Red
- See all platforms where Red's books are sold

Visit Substance B today to learn more about your favorite independent authors.

Printed in the USA
CPSIA information can be obtained
at www.ICGtesting.com
LVHW010327070324
773694LV00012B/323

9 781950 624102